Terror in the Fog

The wind had sharpened and whiplashed Rosemary's cheeks with its chill. She got up and walked up and down the driveway in an effort to keep warm. She kept looking at her wristwatch, wondering why it was taking Drew so long to have walked part way down the road and drive back....But he was coming, she realized at last with a rush of relief.

Then the vehicle came into view. It was not, she saw in horror as it came speeding down the driveway, Drew's small sports car. It was a Volkswagen bus and it was headed directly at her.

She jumped backward onto the grass and it swerved to follow her. She stumbled and fell with rag-doll limpness, her throat locked and all her senses stunned in what she realized were her last few moments of life....

FROM SECRET PLACES
is an original POCKET BOOK edition.

From
Secret Places

by Miriam Lynch

PUBLISHED BY POCKET BOOKS NEW YORK

FROM SECRET PLACES

POCKET BOOK edition published March, 1973

This POCKET BOOK edition includes every word
contained in the original, higher-priced edition. It is printed
from brand-new plates made from completely reset, clear, easy-to-read
type. POCKET BOOK editions are published by POCKET BOOKS, a division
of Simon & Schuster, Inc., 630 Fifth Avenue, New York, N.Y. 10020.
Trademarks registered in the United States and other countries.

Printed in the U.S.A.   Cover art by Bob Abbett.

From
Secret Places

In dead of night with hidden faces
Ghosts come forth from secret places.
(Old verse, author unknown)

Chapter One

ROSEMARY KNEW, the moment she saw Daria at the
door, that this was no ordinary hospital visit. The bouquet
of out-of-season flowers was too big and gaudy and expensive, too blatantly an attempt at reparation for ten days of
neglect.

The flowers hid almost the entire upper half of Daria's
sturdy body and reached to her chin. Her round, beaming
face, with the boyishly cropped hair above it, looked dis-
embodied, elfish, like that of some woodland creature out
of its element.

She came into the room with fawnlike shyness, as
though the slightest sound would send her skittering away.
And Rosemary was not fooled for an instant.

The guilt was not, she knew, because of the fact that
there had been nothing of Daria for almost two weeks except her signature on a card that had come from the girls
in the office, a group card signed by twenty others. There
had not even been a call, although there was a telephone
in her private room.

Daria was smiling, and there was that strange thing
about her. She did not smile because of some happy glow
inside her, or as an expression of friendliness or even of
politeness. Daria smiled when she was nervous or embarrassed or uncertain.

Most of her teeth were showing now. Her lips kept
twitching over them. This time it must be something im-

portant, Rosemary thought, something so agitating that she can not keep her mouth still.

Premonition, faint at first, tightened its hold as Daria dropped the bouquet on the table at the foot of the bed and then sat down with jerky motions.

Her voice was an octave too high when she asked, "How are you, anyway? How much longer do you have to serve? When are they going to spring you?"

She tittered at her own joke and then leaned forward with false interest when Rosemary said that she expected to be able to go home in a couple of days. Mononucleosis, Rosemary explained as though the other girl had been a casual acquaintance and not her roommate for the past year, left one shockingly weak. The doctor had told her that she must rest for another couple of weeks after she was discharged.

That led her to speak of the office. "I imagine they're getting along all right without me? The firm hasn't had to go out of business because I haven't been there?"

It was her own feeble joke, but she wasn't deceived by the stretching of Daria's mouth. The other girl was betrayed by her hands, which kept opening and shutting the clasp of her handbag, making a tiny, metallic sound that fell into a sudden and awkward silence.

Daria said at last, "Oh, everything's fine, just fine! They had to hire a new girl, and she's working out great. The boss is quite impressed. As a matter of fact . . ."

She did not finish the sentence, but Rosemary could guess the rest: If you don't come back, it'll be no great loss. If you're out too long, you may not have a job to come back to. Not the same one, at any rate.

But it wasn't that. There was something else that Daria was trying to say, and her face was puckered with the effort. She was looking over Rosemary's head, staring intently at the bed light.

Well, let's get it over with, Rosemary thought, and asked aloud, "How's Tommy? Have you seen him? He hasn't been in, either. I got just one card from him."

Daria made a swallowing sound. "It happens that I

have. Quite a few times. And if you're sore about us not coming, I'm sorry!"

She did not sound sorry but a little angry and defiant. "We've been busy. Oh, heck! I was going to wait until you were on your feet, but I might as well tell you now. Tommy—well, if you remember, it was me he took out first. And then he sort of got—got infatuated with you. But it couldn't have gone very deep, now, could it? Because he started to come around when you were in here, and it got serious. And we're going to be married!" she burst out in a noisy voice.

Rosemary didn't say anything for a long time. She lay quietly and waited for the pain to come. When it did, it was only the faint twinge of wounded pride.

The thing with Tommy Ross hadn't been much, just an escape from the monotony of a routine job and evenings spent with a girl with whom, she had discovered almost at once, she had little in common.

Tommy had not even been very much fun. He had his own collection of problems and grievances, to which he seemed to have added each time she saw him: lack of appreciation by his employers; slights which she guessed were imagined; tradespeople who overcharged him or gave him poor service. Rosemary had felt sorry for him and mistaken that, for a little while, for love.

Trying to catch Daria's eye, she said, "I hope you'll be very happy. Will it be soon?"

Daria nodded, and the smile came back. "Just as soon as we finish with the blood tests and get the license. What Tommy says is there's no point in us paying the rent on two apartments—his part, that is; you know, he's got a couple of roomies—so we might as well get married right away and save that much money."

That wasn't all of it. Rosemary closed her eyes for a moment, and when she opened them, she was dazzled by the brightness of Daria's teeth.

"He doesn't have any furniture, and of course there's mine. It was my place, after all." The ring of defiance did not match the beaming face. "I knew you'd understand."

Rosemary said wearily, "So you want me to move out.

No problem. The minute I get out of here, I'll make some other arrangements."

Daria sprang out of her chair as suddenly as though it had been wired and someone had turned on an electrical switch. Her face was sober and a little pale with relief.

"We can plan on that, then? Say in a week, at the latest?"

When Daria reached the door, she seemed to feel impelled to say something more. She turned and pointed at the flowers on the table.

"You'd better ring for a nurse to put those in water. No sense in letting them wilt; they cost a small fortune. Not that I begrudge the money. Anything for a friend, I always say."

When she was gone, Rosemary lay listening to the footsteps in the corridor. They were quiet but steady, the subdued tread of hospital visitors. She began to realize how alone and friendless she was in the city she had come to a year before to work and live.

Self-pity would be next, and that, she decided, she did not need. She pulled herself up from her pillow and stretched out a hand, but not to ring for someone to take care of the flowers with their heavy, sickening odor. She pulled open the drawer of the bedside table and took out the letter that had come two days ago.

Aunt Edith's handwriting was a careless scrawl, but Rosemary had managed to decipher the words with some difficulty and now had only to sweep her eyes over them.

"Sorry you could not come for your grandfather's funeral and hope you will be recovered by the time this reaches you. As you see, I'm still at Farview. Soon will be spring, and it is lovely here then. Pay me a visit. Can convalesce. Lonely now, only you and I left."

Henry Gilbert had been an old man. There had been no personal grief for Rosemary in his passing. She did not, in fact, even remember him very well. She had been—she tried to think back—only eight or nine the last time she spent a summer at Farview.

Edith had kept the ties from fraying. She had visited her brother and his wife and his daughter on her way to California when Rosemary was in high school, shortly before her parents' death. There had been sporadic letters. She had asked for snapshots, and Rosemary had sent them. Another invitation had come only a few weeks ago, urgent, almost pleading, bewailing the fact that she had not seen her niece for a long time.

All Rosemary had felt about her grandfather's death was a few moments of sorrow that old age and sickness had chipped away more of what was left of her family. It was as Aunt Edith had written: there were only the two of them remaining—unless you counted Andrew Chester, Edith's stepson, whose father had been her second husband.

Drew Chester. Rosemary had not thought of him for a long time, that teasing, energetic boy who was a few years older than she and who had spent his summers, as Rosemary had for three years, at Farview.

She closed her eyes, and she could see it—that big, isolated house at the end of a peninsula, its many rooms crowded all during the warm weather with guests up from New York and Boston overflowing the lawns, their voices rising to her bedroom in lively conversation and high-pitched laughter.

Thinking back to those sunlit days and the merrymaking at night, she could not remember why, at seven and eight and nine, she had had the vague impression that there was something that made Aunt Edith different from other women. There was her striking beauty: lovely, wide-set dark eyes, camellia skin, cheekbones that were strong and high, a mouth that looked exaggeratedly wide and red.

Farview itself was like the castle of a small girl's dreams. The halls were as big as the apartment Rosemary had shared with Daria. There were ells that were reached by short staircases and a cupola atop the roof which was a tower for a make-believe princess imprisoned in it. When Drew consented to play her childish games with her, they would search for hidden treasure and secret rooms and pirate ships out on the ocean.

After Rosemary's long months of school in a crowded Midwest city, Farview had been like a lazy dream, and she could remember how she wept each time she left the big, weather-silvered house behind, huddling in the back seat of her father's car, angry and feeling the deprivation of what she was losing.

There had been that special odor in the air, the odor of the timeless pine trees and the sea and the first tang of autumn.

Three summers only, for then her mother had slipped into the illness which was to last until her death. And so Farview, on its long finger of land, had been something laid away in Rosemary's memory, to be taken out now and then from its wrapping of time.

She thought of it now, lingeringly and wistfully. She saw in her imagination her great, many-windowed childhood castle, smelled the clean, salty air mingled with the tangy odor of the pine trees, heard the thundering crash of the waves.

It was there waiting for her, and there was no better place on the face of the earth in which to gain back her strength and put together the broken pieces of her life.

Soon it would be spring. She had never seen spring at Farview or in Grist Mill Corners, the little town at the other end of the peninsula. What cleaner and more comforting place could she have found for the period of convalescence the doctor had ordered?

So she went back—back to the place of happy childhood memories. And it wasn't the same.

It wasn't the same at all.

Chapter Two

IT TOOK her only part of a day, once she was out of the hospital, to do everything she had to do before she left: to remove her clothing from the small closet in the small bedroom of the small apartment she had shared with Daria, to pack the things she owned—surprisingly few, because she was not a hoarder—and to call up about her car.

The car had been a mistake, but everyone in the town she lived in before moving to the city had owned a car. It was a way of life; from the age of sixteen on, you simply did not function without one. Rosemary had carried that taken-for-granted attitude with her. The black Pontiac, ten years old then, had eaten its head off in garage fees, and although she had used it only a few times, she still refused to consider selling it because it had belonged to her father.

On that morning in late March, with her suitcases and a carton of books in the trunk and a road map on the front seat beside her, she was thankful for the car. The Pontiac acted like a proper old lady, observing the traffic signs, keeping her tires intact, rising to moderate speed on the highways. But Rosemary found the two-day trip a monotonous grind. When she reached New England, she saw no signs of spring, despite what the calendar said. The ground looked like iron. There were patches of snow, dirty and crusty, at the edges of the roads, and the trees, stripped of their leaves, showed the bones of their branches. The sky seemed indecisive, alternately dropping a fine, cold drizzle and then breaking apart for brief spells of watery sunlight.

It had been threatening to rain all day, and at two o'clock, when Rosemary came to the outskirts of Grist Mill Corners, the heavy downpour began. She felt as though she were moving into a strange country, for the little town looked abandoned and bleak. The summer hotels, old, gray houses that seemed quaint in the sunlight, were shuttered, their out-of-date porch furniture gone, and the signs on their lawns were faded.

The gift shops and refreshment stands were boarded up. Only in one little store, on this wet, murky day, did a light shine through the veil of rain. Rosemary remembered it: it had been a sort of general store, preserving its other-era atmosphere for the delight of summer visitors. She could remember the briny smell of a pickle barrel and the display of penny candy behind cloudy glass, the cans of food on the shelves, the cooking utensils and fishing equipment and straw hats and even sunbonnets in a jumble on the counter.

Rosemary found a space and pulled the car up against the curb. Parking was no problem at this time of the year; in the middle of the season, it was impossible. On Sunday mornings when she was a child, she had sometimes been allowed to drive into town with Aunt Edith's guests when they came to buy the bulky out-of-town newspapers.

They used to buy her overwhelmingly large bags of penny candy, pinwheels, colored dots on long strips of paper, licorice whips, sour balls, peppermint drops. These she would conscientiously take back to Farview and share with Drew, who would have disdained to press his fourteen-year-old nose against a candy counter but did condescend to eat his portion—and sometimes most of hers as well.

As she got out of the car, Rosemary smiled at the memory of those enchanted Sunday mornings. Her throat was dry from the long ride, and she had not stopped for lunch. The sour balls would ease the dryness; she did not want to be hoarse and croaking when she met her aunt for the first time after all these years. Running through the rain and pulling open the store's storm door, she did not notice at first that this was not the dim, dusty place of her childhood.

The brightness of the fluorescent lights dazzled her. Then, when her vision adjusted to it, she saw that the interior of the store had been painted. The walls were brilliantly white. A soda fountain stretched where the cluttered counter had been. The penny candy display was gone. There was no pickle barrel, and where the round little stove had stood there was a counter of cheap plastic toys, alarm clocks, sunglasses, and bathing caps. There was a newspaper and magazine rack against one wall and shelves full of cosmetics. Nothing was the same as it had been fourteen years before.

"Help you, Miss?"

The woman was behind the soda fountain, a cheerful, elderly woman with her hair cut in the latest fashion. Rosemary could not remember whether or not she had ever seen her before, did not know whether she had always been the proprietor of the store and had been renovated with it or whether she was a stranger lately come to Grist Mill Corners.

"Something I can do for you?"

Her disappointment still lingering, Rosemary climbed up onto a stool. The coffee in the Silex container looked good, black and strong. There was a stack of sandwiches wrapped in waxed paper on the counter.

While the woman poured the coffee into a mug and put one of the sandwiches on a plate, she focused part of her attention on Rosemary. Her eyes, a pale, faded blue behind her oversized granny glasses, kept darting in the girl's direction. And when she could no longer bear not knowing, she asked, "Where are you from?"

Rosemary told her and added, because she knew what the next question would be, "I'm on my way to Farview. I spent three summers here when I was a kid."

The word "Farview" seemed to effect some sort of magic over the woman, releasing a spate of words so swift and unrestrained and flowing that she almost stuttered over them. She spoke of Edith Gilbert, changing the last name to Chester in apologetic correction, and how she had always been a little in awe of the lady of the big house. She sighed over the old days, when Farview had been crowded each summer with Mrs. Chester's fancy friends from the city. "Fancy" was the word she used. She mourned the passing of those summers of years ago when every weekend had poured money into the store.

"All gone now. Maybe it was her father being sick, and she had to give up the parties. Now he's gone, too, buried only a few weeks ago. Nobody up there except her—the lady—and that stepson of hers. Nobody else. Once in a while she has company, but they come and go. Don't stop in here at all," she added on an aggrieved note. "Just her and him, the young man, for the past month or so." Two things out of all the chattering impressed themselves on Rosemary's mind. First, that Drew Chester was staying— perhaps living permanently?—with his stepmother, although Edith's letter had stressed that she was "lonely" and given the impression that she was alone at Farview. And second, Rosemary learned that there was no truth to the popular idea that New Englanders were taciturn and unfriendly.

The telephone rang when she was almost ready for her second cup of coffee, and the woman went to answer it. She did not come back for a long time. Rosemary heard one side of a conversation about some sort of church activity, which included what seemed like an endless listing of committee members and volunteers.

Ever since she first began to drink coffee, she'd had the habit of having a second cup to follow the first, and so she remained sitting at the counter. When she heard nothing to make her hopeful that the woman at the telephone would hang up the receiver soon, she got down from the stool and wandered about the store. She went to the newspaper rack and took out an edition of a Boston paper.

Its headlines were as depressing as usual: a strike, a bombing, a fatal accident, and a spectacular jewel robbery. There were a couple of paragraphs on the front page about the recent disappearance of one of the world's richest men, Martin Morse.

Rosemary was not particularly interested in Martin Morse, millionaire recluse whose eccentricities were far removed from her own sphere. But she read through the front-page account of his disappearance and then turned to the spillover on an inside page. There was not much new in any of it; she read about his disappearance merely to pass the time.

The story was padded with paragraphs about other well-known figures who had vanished and never been seen again. They, too, seemed unreal and remote, characters in a story she had read a long time ago.

The woman finally returned to the counter. Rosemary had her second cup of coffee, paid for the luncheon and the paper, and went back to her car. The rain had almost completely stopped, but the narrow road that led to the house at the end of the peninsula held puddles in its pot-holes, and the waves that hurled themselves up on either side of it boomed in a heavy rhythm which sounded some-how menacing.

With its upper stories lost in the mist, Farview looked like a house that had been partially destroyed. Its windows were cloudy in the gloom. The rain had drenched its shin-gles and turned them dark. And as she drove slowly through the lane that led to the front door, Rosemary saw that the long grass was flattened, the shrubbery overgrown and shapeless, the flagstones of the walk almost hidden by the weeds growing between the slick pieces of stone.

She got out of the car, not caring or even noticing that the drizzle was cold and pervasive, and looked up at the place which had been so gracious and impressive when she had seen it last. She saw the deterioration of age and ne-glect in the sagging of the porch balustrades, a cracked windowpane, the missing spokes in the elaborate ginger-bread trimming over the entrance.

Somewhere inside, a light was burning on this gloomy afternoon. That faint, misty shine was all that kept Far-view from seeming deserted, a place whose occupants had gone away and left it to be battered by the elements.

She took her suitcases from the trunk of the car and started up the steps. They groaned under her feet with a sound that was almost like the voice of a human being in pain. The front door looked inhospitable and forbidding. But then it opened, and Edith Chester came rushing through it, across the porch and out into the water drip-ping from the gutter of the overhanging eave.

She did not seem to care that she was directly under the dirty downpour and that her hair, as black and beautifully shiny as it had ever been, was becoming soaked. Her arms were thrown out in a gesture of welcome that was somehow theatrical, and she gathered her niece into them, hugged the girl close to her, and cried, in a voice that was like light and silvery music, "Darling! Darling! You've come at last! I'm so very, very glad to see you!"

Edith had always been extravagant in her speech, made ordinary things into small dramas, swept the others around her into her own easily kindled excitement. Now Rosemary felt the magic again. Just for that moment while she was in Edith Chester's embrace. Then, during the little flurry of activity that followed it—Edith taking one of the suitcases from her, opening the door with her free hand, and leading her into the hall—she felt a little twinge of puzzlement.

She could not have hoped for a warmer welcome. She could accept Edith's exaggerated mannerisms as part of the woman's nature. But there had been something else, something that went beyond those things. What she had heard in her aunt's voice and did not understand was relief.

But why, Rosemary asked herself, should Edith be relieved to have me here in Farview? It did not make sense. She could not be all that lonely—not if Drew were here with her. Perhaps she had been worried about my traveling alone in such miserable weather. Her imagination—and high-strung people like Edith Chester must have overactive imaginations—had probably pictured me in an accident on the slick, fog-veiled roads, Rosemary decided.

"Two suitcases!" Edith was fluting. "Which means that you're going to make a nice, long visit. You don't know how glad I am, you dear, sweet child! No!" she ordered as Rosemary tried to speak. "I don't want to hear any talk about when you're leaving. We're not going to even mention that. Because I shall feel sorry for myself, alone here with just the two women. You must remember them—

Bertha and Lucinda Swift. Hired girls, they call themselves."

Rosemary, who had been about to say that everything she owned was in the suitcases and the cardboard carton in the car trunk, found her thoughts diverted in another direction.

She did not remember the two women Edith had spoken about. There had been servants in Farview during her childhood summers, but she had had a vague impression that they were a little family group: a cook, who insisted on having "Mrs." prefixed to her name; the woman's daughter who had done the serving and the upstairs work, and the woman's husband, the handyman and gardener.

There was presumably no man-of-all-work now, not with the grounds overrun and neglected as they were. That was one of the unexplained things, but Rosemary could not bring herself to ask any questions on that subject. And smothering all those thoughts came the puzzlement about why Edith had not mentioned her stepson.

She asked aloud, "But isn't Drew here?"

"For the time being. He will be leaving, I think, within a short time."

The sound of musical bells was missing in Edith's voice. It had in it a note of hardness, almost harshness.

And that was the most puzzling thing of all.

Chapter Three

"What makes you ask?" Edith suddenly demanded. "He didn't—he didn't write to you, did he? How did you know he was staying here?"

She seemed agitated. Her mouth, the frosty pink lipstick

on it too thick and heavy for its size, seemed to twitch out the words. Her face looked a little pale in the cloudy light from the chandelier above their heads.

Rosemary explained about the woman in the little store in Grist Mill Corners.

"They know everything, those villagers. They have nothing else to do in the off-season months but exchange gossip. It's always been like that. We're their favorite topic."

She hesitated for a moment and then, reaching down for the suitcase again, asked, "What else did she say, that odious woman?"

"Nothing much." Rosemary's mind went racing backward. "Not anything of importance, at any rate."

She wanted to ask what difference it could make, how it could matter if a woman of few interests and natural curiosity had talked about Farview and the people in it. But Edith was moving ahead, walking purposefully toward the staircase at the far end of the shadowed hall—walking hastily, as though if they hurried past them, Rosemary would not see the faded wallpaper or the banisters grown dull from want of polishing or the empty niches at the turns of the stairs.

Once those little recesses had held small pieces of statuary. Once the steps had been covered with thick, soft carpeting. Now that, too, was frayed, worn with age, as was everything else in this once-lovely place.

Rosemary's room was near the head of the staircase on the second floor. That, at least, showed some signs of care. The curtains were crisp and freshly laundered. There was a new coverlet on the bed, its pale pink color matching a shag rug which did not look as though it had ever been walked on. The furniture, bird's-eye maple and a little out-of-date, had not been replaced. But Rosemary had no feeling of coming into a familiar place.

It would take time, she told herself. The uneasiness would go away before long. She was engrossed with those thoughts, not listening to what Edith was saying until a certain phrase penetrated her mind.

". . . the East wing on this floor. You know, at the end of the hall."

Pleasant memories came back when Edith spoke of the ell. Rosemary and Drew had wandered about in that dark area whose doors were closed against young intruders, had searched for secret rooms and hidden treasures and made up ghost stories in its shadowy halls.

"If you don't mind," Edith said, "you'll have to keep out of there. It's in shockingly bad repair—has been since the last hurricane—and, my dear, is actually dangerous. The additions, of course, were built long after the main structure was erected, and built flimsily. Another bad storm could shake them from their foundations."

Then why isn't something done about that? Rosemary wondered. She was still trying to reconcile Farview and shabbiness. In her memory she had always seen it as luxurious—even, in certain areas, sumptuous. Thirteen years ago, she had been too young to think about money—how much was needed to maintain a house this size, and where the money came from. She had merely taken it for granted that her grandfather was rich.

"So you will stay out of there, won't you?" Edith said urgently. "We don't want any accidents."

And then she smiled the beaming, wonderful smile that lit up her face as though a dazzling light shone behind it.

"Now that I have you here again, I don't want anything to happen to you, darling!"

Her arm lifted and fell in a dramatic gesture. "Rest for a while, do! How exhausted you must be after such a long drive, scarcely out of your sickbed as you are! I shall see you later. Dinner is at seven."

Rosemary had read about people sweeping out of a room, but she had never seen it done before. Edith, her movements graceful and fluid, seemed to float away. The skirt of her long dress swayed as she walked. She left the scent of expensive perfume behind her in the air.

When she had finished unpacking, Rosemary went to the window and looked out. The rain had stopped, but it had not taken away with it any of the dismal look of the grounds. The bare branches of the trees were blackened

by the wetness, and the grass and the bushes looked
drenched.

Although there was nothing to see, she remained there,
trying to free herself from the feeling of uneasiness and
disappointment that depressed her spirits.

Her car was still down there in the driveway, and she
began to worry about the possibility of more rain, which
might soak its wires and make it impossible to start. There
was a garage—actually, a converted carriage house—at
the other end of the driveway, which undoubtedly sheltered whatever cars belonged to the members of the
household. Perhaps, she thought, there would be room for
hers there.

She put on her raincoat again and a plastic bandana
over her hair. When she reached the hall, she stopped
short. Looking back at the door that closed off the ell on
that side of the house, she was convinced that she could not
be hearing what she thought she heard.

Yet muffled voices were coming from behind that
closed door. She could not be mistaken. She could not distinguish any particular tones in them, couldn't tell whether
they were masculine or feminine from that distance. She
only knew that someone—several someones, because
there were different shadings and inflections—was in that
ell, which Edith had warned her against as being "dangerous."

The two women who Edith had said were all there was
of the servant staff? Rosemary recalled their names with
some difficulty: Bertha and Lucinda Swift. She was supposed to have remembered them but had not, and did not
now.

She told herself that they were the ones who were talking together in the place she had been cautioned against
entering. She was letting herself get foolishly upset about a
trifling thing, and she started down the hall again trying to
banish it from her mind.

But when she reached the first floor and hesitated there
at the foot of the staircase, she heard the clatter of pots
and pans and dishes coming from the kitchen. And she
knew that this was exactly the way it should have been—

the two women who called themselves hired girls beginning, at this time of day, the preparations for dinner.

Rosemary's footsteps lagged as she opened the front door and started across the porch. From somewhere beyond the driveway, she heard the drone of a car motor. It grew louder as the car came into sight, and she saw the low-slung sports model, gleaming and polished by the wetness, its windshield wipers still racing.

It stopped with a faint screech directly behind her Pontiac, and a man in a black raincoat unfolded himself out of it. He came striding toward the steps and then stopped. There was only a single moment when Rosemary's mind groped for recognition. Then she cried, "Drew?"

He had not changed very much. The blunt features that had given him a slightly belligerent look were somewhat softened. His eyes were still the cleanest, clearest gray she had ever seen. His hair was different—worn longer, but slightly tousled as always. The attractive little boy had grown to extremely good-looking manhood.

She said, as he came slowly up the steps, "I guess you don't remember me!" She was feeling embarrassed over her hard scrutiny, and because he was now studying her with a long, probing stare. "We were playmates . . . oh, a long time ago!"

"Of course I remember you."

His voice had deepened, and in spite of the stoniness in his eyes, it was pleasant and almost gentle. But she stiffened at his next words.

"Why are you here?"

He had always been blunt and disturbingly honest, she remembered. Edith had painstakingly taught him to be mannerly, but she had been unable to curb the unruly tongue and the sometimes unbridled utterances.

He asked again, "What brings you here?"

Rosemary felt the scald of heat in her cheeks and heard the stuttering note in her voice. "Well, that's a fine welcome!" She tried to speak lightly and failed. "I came because Aunt Edith invited me. I've been sick."

Good Lord, that sounds like whining! she realized. And why should I have to explain or apologize?

"I was in the hospital when Grandfather died, so I couldn't, of course, come to the funeral. And then, when I got better . . ."

She was not going to go into that. In another moment, in spite of her determination not to try to justify her presence in Farview, she'd be telling him about Daria and Tommy Ross and her homeless, and possibly jobless, state.

But Drew had interrupted her at any rate. "Ah, yes," he said, with a dipping motion of his head. "Your grandfather! And what did you expect to find, my fair Rose? That you had become an heiress? That part of all this," and he gestured toward the house, "was going to fall into your hot little hands?"

The heat in her face had become more intense, and her voice was caught somewhere in her throat.

"Blushing, Rosemary?" Drew sounded amused. "Do you know you're the only girl I've ever met who can blush? I remember when you were a kid, you'd turn red at the least little thing. Oh, don't turn away!"

He put a hand under her chin and forced her to look at him. He said in a soft, thoughtful voice, "Now who'd have expected it? You weren't a pretty kid. Your eyes were too big for your face and you had flyaway hair, and when I knew you, some of your front teeth were missing, and you were small for your age. But you've improved—yes, indeed! You've grown into a beautiful young woman."

The abrupt change from what had sounded like a faint sneer to what would have been admiration coming from another man left her confused. She knew well enough how she looked. At twenty-two, she had a fragile, delicate prettiness that was somewhat old fashioned. There was about her a freshness that made her seem younger than her years. The flyaway hair that Drew remembered, dark blonde that turned pale gold under bright lights, had been tamed and cut and shaped, and the eyes that had been too large for her face now seemed only widely spaced.

She did not know what to say, so she remained silent. Then Drew had another change of mood. He removed his hand from her chin and seemed to be talking to himself as he said, "I wonder why. Strange; very strange! She doesn't seem to have all that family feeling."

He came back from his absorption with his own thoughts when she complained, "I haven't the slightest idea what you're talking about! And your car is blocking the way to the garage."

"That yours?" He glanced over his shoulder at it. "Give me the keys, and I'll take care of it. May be a tight squeeze with Edith's big old crate taking up so much room in there."

There were things she wanted to ask him. What had happened to Farview to change it from the stately place of their childhood into a run-down relic of its former affluence? Why did he and Edith speak of each other with such apparent lack of affection? What kept him in this remote place, where a man his age would find no form of recreation or career opportunities? How long did he intend to stay?

But Drew's face had a closed, forbidding look about it. She had always been a little in awe of him when they were children, easily upset by his teasing and occasional rudeness.

His remark about her grandfather had been flavored by something that came close to cruelty. She had never even considered the matter of an inheritance. If she had, she would naturally have concluded that whatever Henry Gilbert had left behind would be Edith's, for she was his only surviving child. If he had left a will—and Rosemary supposed that he had—it was doubtful that there was any mention of her name in it. She remembered him only as a quiet, abstracted old man—old and in poor health even thirteen years ago—who had kept to his room most of the time and did not take part in any of his daughter's entertaining. It was doubtful that he ever thought much about Rosemary, either, or was aware of her presence in Farview most of the time.

What Drew had said was ugly. She'd had no plans about monetary things when she'd decided to visit Aunt Edith. The words still rankled, and she handed him the car keys without speaking.

Then she went back into the house, where she was to
spend the strangest and most disturbing night she had yet
known.

Chapter Four

SHE WAS changing her clothes for dinner when she
heard the footsteps passing her door. She thought that perhaps someone was coming to tell her that the others were
waiting downstairs for her, but when she looked at her
watch, she saw that it was only quarter to seven.

Holding the watch against her ear, she went to the door
and opened it. There was no one in her part of the corridor. When she looked in the other direction, she saw a
shadowy figure at the door of the ell. It disappeared as the
door opened and the woman—she was sure it had been a
woman carrying a tray—went through it.

In that brief glimpse, Rosemary had seen a dim glint of
light on a silver coffee pot and covered dishes. She knew
now that she had not been mistaken earlier. In spite of
what Edith had said about the ell being unsafe, someone
was in it—someone whose voice she had heard, and who
was undoubtedly being served his or her dinner at this very
moment.

She stepped back into the room when she heard the
door of the ell open and close. She left her own ajar and
moved to a place where she could see through it.

The woman who passed it without looking in a moment
later was tall and severely dressed in the striped uniform
of a housemaid. Her long skirt was stiffly starched, and it
made a barely audible whisper as she walked. Her hair
was dragged back from her face and fastened in a dough-
nut-shaped knot atop her head. At her side she held an

empty tray, which caught streaks of light as she swung it in her hand.

There was nothing furtive in her manner as she strode past the open door. Her footsteps were firm and unhurried as she went down the staircase.

It was downright silly, Rosemary told herself, to be making a mystery of something that was probably nothing of the kind. It might be that the sister of the woman she had seen was occupying a room in what were probably the servants' quarters. The other maid was probably sick and had to have her meals served to her in her bedroom.

No doubt this was something that had an explanation. All she had to do was ask a simple question of Edith or Drew Chester. Drew, forthright and painfully honest at times, would not hesitate to tell her who was occupying the ell.

But when Rosemary went downstairs, she found only Edith at the table in the breakfast room.

"I thought," she said, "that it might be more pleasant here, since there's just the two of us."

The breakfast room, like every other place in Farview it seemed, looked depressingly dreary. Beyond its French windows was a wide lawn, hidden now by the darkness, which stretched to a ledge that hung above the ocean. Heavy waves smashed against the rocks making a dismal sound in the night.

Edith seemed to be engrossed in her own thoughts, and when Rosemary finally put a question to her, it was not the one she had intended to ask.

"Where's Drew?"

Edith said with a sigh, "Heaven only knows. He may have gone into town and had a hamburger or a frankfurter there. We don't see much of each other. Sometimes he's gone for days at a time."

Rosemary had not intended to ask the next question, but it seemed to pop out without volition.

"Why?"

The woman shrugged her shoulders and said, "Who knows? He tells me nothing."

There was something aggrieved in the tone of her voice.

And under it, a sound of nervousness. Why Edith's nerves should stretch tautly because of anything concerning Drew, Rosemary could not guess. She had always seemed fond of her stepson, had remained patient when he got into one of his boyish scrapes, had been able to talk to him and about him.

"Perhaps he gets bored here," Rosemary offered. "There can't be much of anything for him to do. Does he intend to stay long, do you know?"

"I have no idea."

Edith sounded a little snappish, and seemed not to want to go on with the subject. She began to speak about her father, explaining that he had scarcely left his bedroom during the last years of his life. She said that his death had been a release, and so she had not been able to grieve for him.

That brought back to Rosemary's mind what Drew had said about an inheritance. Of course, the house and whatever Henry Gilbert had left must belong to Edith now. Must, and should. She had been a devoted daughter, nursing him through long years of sickness and the painful days preceding his death, giving up her own social activities because he had needed constant attention.

The picture of Edith as a dedicated sickroom angel was shattered suddenly. "But we mustn't talk of sad things tonight. You can't bring back the past by talking of it. Tell me what your life was like until now. We didn't see much of each other for such a long time. Even that time I stopped over on my way to the West Coast was much too short for us to become reacquainted."

This was the Edith that Rosemary remembered, her face lively, wanting to be amused. Drew, Rosemary thought, could not have a monopoly on boredom. What could her aunt find to divert her here in this isolated place? Now that her father was dead, there could be no reason for her to stay on in Farview. She seemed to be the restless, pleasure-seeking type. How had she endured the snow-locked house during the long winter months?

Rosemary had carefully and tactfully formed a question, but one of the servants came in with a fresh pot of coffee at that moment. This was the one Edith called "Bertha," and had she not designated her by name, Rosemary wouldn't have known which of the Swift women she was. They looked alike, both tall and slim to the point of gauntness. But when the other sister came in to clear the plates away while Bertha poured the coffee, Rosemary, seeing them together, realized that they were not twins.

Bertha was the one who had carried food into the second-floor ell and then left with a tray in her hand. She had a stronger nose, a thinner mouth, a forehead that bulged more prominently than her sister's. She was, too, the more dominant of the two. Lucinda had the softer face, and might have been pretty if she had not worn her hair in that unattractive snatched-back arrangement.

Rosemary's nice little theory about one of the hired girls being ill and her sister waiting on her went a-glimmering. The two sturdy women both appeared to be in excellent health. Then who was in that part of the house which was supposed to be empty? Rosemary wondered.

She studied the backs of the two women as they went out in the direction of the kitchen. She had a strange feeling about them. They were too precisely the prototype of New England hired help: the tight, unsmiling mouths, the starchiness in both manner and clothing, the proudly held heads, and the twangy, no-nonsense voices. Call it sixth sense—and actually, that *is* all it is, she thought.

Rosemary had seen all there was to see about them, but she wasn't sure that when she saw one of them alone again she would be able to tell whether it was Lucinda or Bertha.

Pushing aside her plate, Edith cut into Rosemary's thoughts by saying, "I'm going to be very strict with you, dear child. If you like, you can take a little walk, and then it's bed for you, darling. You've had a long, exhausting day. All that driving must have been a terrific strain. And I don't want to have to worry about your having a relapse. I wouldn't want that on my conscience."

"Take a walk" Rosemary said uncertainly. "After dark, and alone?"

Edith's laugh was like a set of chimes sounding as

though someone with a tiny hammer was hitting them and producing light music.

"My little city mouse! There's no danger here. We're safer than we would be anywhere in the world. No crime can find us in this secluded place. Who could come up the road from the village except by car? It's a good three miles. The tides come high on either side of it, and after a rainstorm the ground is full of puddles. What I mean is that this is not the ideal spot for a burglar or some small-time thief."

Rosemary could agree to the logic in that, but it did not make her any more eager to go wandering around the grounds and slough through the wet grass and the untidy paths.

"Maybe I'll skip that part of it," she told Edith, "and just go to bed with a book, read myself to sleep."

Edith repeated vaguely, "A book?" as though she had never heard the word before.

So her aunt was not a reader, and Rosemary wondered once more what in the world she did find to amuse herself with during the quiet days and long evenings at Farview. Without companionship—for it had been all too evident in the things she had said about Drew that there was no friendliness between them—she should have been utterly bored.

Rosemary was about to bring up that subject, but Edith was out of her chair now and moving toward the door. She stopped there long enough to say, "There's your grandfather's den. You should be able to find something to read in there."

What Rosemary found in that airless little room, which smelled as though no windows in it had been opened for years, were dusty classics on half-filled shelves and a few old romantic novels, which had evidently been left behind by Edith's guests a good many years ago. None of the authors were familiar, but Rosemary picked out two books and carried them back to her room. When she was in bed and had turned on the lamp beside it, she was annoyed to find that the light bulb was a low-watt one and that, unless she wanted to risk straining her eyes, she was not going to be able to read a single page.

This small, senseless economy both puzzled and surprised her. Remembering the lavishness of Edith's weekend parties—buffet suppers for twenty or more guests, extra servants hired for the occasions, even orchestras brought in from a city miles away—this thing about the low-watt bulb seemed to symbolize the changes that had taken place in Farview.

Rosemary didn't have long to wonder about the contrast between that apparently affluent way of life and the lack of even the slightest sign of luxury in the house as it was now. She was asleep within fifteen minutes after climbing into bed.

When she awakened, everything in the room was smothered in complete darkness, and her mind groped for an instant or two before she remembered where she was. The sound of the ocean was like the rumbling of thunder. But she had fallen asleep to its steady rhythm, and knew that it was not that which had dragged her up from dreamless oblivion. She had a vague feeling that someone had screamed.

She sat up and leaned forward, her ears straining. What she heard then was a series of low groans, soft at first, then rising in volume until they were full and loud and anguished.

Somewhere, someone in the house must be in pain. That was the only thought in Rosemary's mind as she reached to turn the bed lamp on. She threw back the bedcovers and got out of bed, found her dressing robe and put it on, and slid her feet into slippers.

When she reached the door and opened it, she was able to hear the groaning more clearly. It was coming from beyond the staircase, from one of the rooms along that other stretch of corridor. Why had no one else come to find the source of that tormented sound and do something about it? Edith's bedroom, too, was in that part of the house, Rosemary remembered. Drew slept up on the third floor, where he had a second room for his seashell collection and his homemade equipment for scientific experiments—all jealously guarded.

"And why he hasn't blown us sky-high before this, I shall never know," Edith had once said cheerfully.

Rosemary ran along the hall, passed the staircase, and stopped because the moaning was growing fainter. She hesitated with her hand around the knob of the first door she came to. This was the bedroom her grandfather had occupied. She had been in it once or twice during those bygone summers, making brief, polite visits to the man who had seemed very old to her even then and was seldom seen on the first floor.

She turned the knob, pushed open the door, and went over the threshold. There was a dim night light burning, and at first the room seemed to be filled with only shadows.

Then outlines began to emerge. She saw the huge bed against the far wall and the man who lay against the pillows with his eyes closed, quiet now, scarcely seeming to be breathing.

Rosemary recognized him, but she told herself that she must be in the midst of a hideous dream. For the man in the bed could not be her grandfather; Henry Gilbert was dead.

Chapter Five

STUNNED WITH shock, she moved backward and crashed into the open door. She was conscious of a twinge of pain, but her gaze remained riveted on the man in the bed. He had not stirred when the old door hinges squawked. He lay with his eyes closed, his hair as white as the pillow behind his head.

Of course she recognized him. She could not have mistaken that face, with its sharp beak of a nose, the stern mouth, the sharply-carved chin and cheekbones, for that of anyone else.

But Henry Gilbert was dead. His funeral had coincided with the day she had been admitted to the hospital. Edith, Drew, the woman in the village store—all of them had spoken of his death.

Rosemary turned and fled through the door, her hand automatically going out to pull it shut behind her. She raced past the staircase, and when she reached her own room, still dazed and shaking, she went to the bed and sat down on its edge.

She remained there for a long time. Her mind was in chaos, and dozens of little hammers seemed to be beating in her head.

She sat there until exhaustion overwhelmed her. Then she lay back on the bed and slept, still in her robe and slippers, sinking into a dark pit that closed in over her and closed out the horror.

She was awake early in the morning and waited for a long time before getting up. The memory of what she had seen in that room at the other side of the staircase was vivid in her mind and possessed all her thoughts.

It had not been a dream; she was certain of that. The man in the room who lay in that big, old bed and moaned in the dark hours of the night from the infirmities of old age and the illness that consumed his body, *had* been Henry Gilbert.

When Rosemary heard the sounds of the house coming awake—footsteps on the staircase, voices somewhere on the first floor—she got up and dressed. She went along the corridor, merely glancing at the closed door of Henry Gilbert's room, and stopped in front of her aunt's.

Edith sang out, "Just a minute, darling!" and her footsteps came rushing across the room. "So early you are, dear child!"

She stood framed in the doorway, hair arranged meticulously, makeup artfully applied. She looked a little uncertain as she stepped back to admit Rosemary, and her voice was flattened as she asked, "What is it? You look so strange, so disturbed!"

Rosemary said, "And with good reason!"

Her aunt's room—boudoir was what it was, actually— was much the same as it had been when Rosemary had seen it last. Everything in it was a pale yellow, like faded sunlight; draperies and rugs and the skirt of the dressing table and the upholstery of its stool. The French provincial bed and highboy had once been white and gold, but the years had dimmed and yellowed them so that all the furnishings were almost the same color.

Only part of Rosemary's attention was engaged by her surroundings. She was looking directly into Edith's face as she said, "I saw Grandfather last night."

Edith moved easily to the dressing table and sat down in front of it. On its surface were dozens of jars and bottles, and above them her face was quiet and intent, the face of a priestess worshipping her own beauty. When she lifted her eyes to meet Rosemary's in the mirror, they were as cool as though she had not heard what the girl had said.

Rosemary repeated it, more loudly this time and with every word spaced for emphasis.

"We were talking about him," Edith said sympathetically. "That happens often, doesn't it? Something you say or hear remains in your subconscious mind and then comes out as a dream when you're asleep."

"But it wasn't a dream!" She wished that Edith would turn around. Speaking to a reflection gave the conversation the effect of unreality. "He was there, in his bedroom." She half turned and gestured toward the door. "Aunt Edith, I was not mistaken, nor having a nightmare, nor imagining things. I heard him groaning. He sounded as though he were in pain. And when I went in—when I went in, I saw him lying in bed. I recognized him at once."

Edith swung around on the stool then. She arose from it, stretched out her hands, and clasped them around Rosemary's.

"My dear, I am so very sorry that something upset you on your first night here. That was what it was, I'm sure.

Being in a strange place, in an unfamiliar bed. The mind plays peculiar tricks sometimes. I'm sure you believe that it was all real," she added in a kindly manner. "But you must see how impossible that could have been."

"I only know what I saw," Rosemary said stubbornly. "I think it must have been the groaning that awakened me, although I'm not too sure about that. But I did hear it, and I got up and put on my robe and slippers, and I went down the hall . . ."

She broke off because Edith's face was wearing an expression of affectionate concern. "Darling child," she said, "you are beginning to worry me. You didn't take anything before you went to bed, a sleeping pill that made you hallucinate or something like that? I know it's common among young people today. Drugs and barbiturates, used the way my generation used liquor . . ."

Rosemary interrupted her with a harsh, outraged cry. "Of course not! Aunt Edith, I tell you I actually saw him!"

"But my father is dead," Edith said gently. "It happened more than two weeks ago. It was a very quiet death. He had slipped into a coma a few days before and slept away without having awakened from it."

With her hand still around the girl's, she led her in the direction of the door. "Come, I'll show you that there's no one in that room and could not have been."

Henry Gilbert's bedroom was empty. A rug was rolled up and leaning against one wall. The chairs and dressers were covered by sheets, giving them the appearance of crouching ghosts. The bed was stripped and its mattress was exposed.

Rosemary stood at the threshold, her mind befogged with puzzlement and her heart beating with hard, uneven strokes. Moments went by before she could speak again, and when she did, her voice came out in a squeak.

"But I know I saw him here last night. I did!"

She sounded like a stubborn, petulant child, and when she turned to look at Edith, she saw on the woman's face only an indulgent smile.

"Darling, you're not convinced yet, are you? It must

have been a very vivid dream. Perhaps you'd feel better if I told you more about it. Come back to my room. Being here is not . . . pleasant. There are too many memories, and I have not . . . have not quite got over losing my father."

Rosemary's brain was still spinning with bewilderment but a little twist of remorse came into it. When they were in Edith's bedroom again, she said, "I'm sorry that I've upset you. Maybe we'd better not talk about it anymore."

"But I want to. If I tell you how it was, you may feel better."

She began to speak of Henry Gilbert's last hours, of the long bedside vigil and the doctor who had come from Grist Mill Corners to make the pronouncement of death. She described the funeral to Rosemary, small and private because the man had had few friends left and had not known many of the townspeople.

"He is buried in the churchyard in the village. I haven't had time to order a headstone, so the grave is unmarked as yet. But if you like, dear child, you can drive down there, and I'm sure someone in charge will point it out to you."

"Perhaps I will do that," Rosemary murmured. "Just to convince myself."

The idea took hold then and became stronger during the morning hours when she had nothing else to occupy her mind. There was nothing, she discovered, nothing at all to do in this remote place. Farview, the only house on the peninsula, had no neighbors. Storms and high tides could literally isolate it, flooding the road which was the only means of getting back to the village.

It was no day to sit out on the lawn and soak up sunlight, which was what Rosemary had thought about doing when she made up her mind to come to Farview. But she had seen Farview with false vision, remembering the sundrenched days of her childhood summers: she had packed into one of her suitcases dark glasses and a bathing suit. And I must have been out of my mind, she thought wryly. Summer came late to Maine. Late March was no time for sunbathing.

Nor was this the sort of day to go poking about in a cemetery. The ragged clouds hung low, and a sharp wind was tossing the bare trees. The waves at the foot of the cliff crashed and fell back snarling.

But after lunch, still uncertain and puzzling, she put a sweater on under her all-weather coat and went to the coach house for her car. There were only two of them in that dim and ill-smelling place, her own and the big, black limousine that presumably belonged to Edith. Drew's flashy sports model was nowhere in sight, and Rosemary wondered about him, about what he found to do in this dismal place and why he was here at all when he and Edith did not seem to be on good terms.

Rosemary had not seen him at either breakfast or lunch, and Edith had not mentioned him or explained his absence. And Rosemary did not want to bring up the subject, since her aunt had seemed perturbed when she asked about him the night before.

She had only a short time to think about Edith and Drew and the other strange features of the house she was leaving behind, because the wind was buffeting the car and all her strength and all her attention had to be centered on keeping it on the road. She came to the little village with a sigh of relief. As she drove down its one street, with most of its houses shuttered and all but one of its stores boarded up, she came to a small, brown-shingled church with a tiny graveyard beside it.

It was a very old cemetery. Some of its headstones tilted at sharp angles; others had crumbled so that the carving on them was obliterated. But the brown grass was neatly clipped and the walks were clear. She was walking through them, trying to remember the directions Edith had given her, when a door opened at the side of the church and a very old man came through it.

He wore clerical garb and a Roman collar and held a breviary in one frail hand. When he came abreast of Rosemary, he said in a cracked voice, "Good afternoon. I'm the rector, Father Lyman. May I help you, my dear?"

Rosemary realized that he must have been hard of hearing, because he had turned his head and bent one side of it toward her as he waited for her to speak.

She lifted her own voice to a pitch that was higher than its normal one and told him her name. "I'm looking for my grandfather's grave. He died a little more than two weeks ago."

"Ah, yes! He went to his rest on the fifteenth of the month."

The eyes of the Anglican priest, weak and faded, looked sad. Rosemary guessed that the sadness was not only for the loss of a parishioner, but also for the many others he had lost through the years—and, perhaps, the knowledge that his own years on earth were few.

He motioned to Rosemary to follow him, and they went down a path which led to a group of graves around a twisted oak tree. One of them looked new, its mound of dirt still high and black.

Father Lyman stopped there and pointed with a hand that was not quite steady.

"His mortal remains," he said gently. "I am certain that his soul is in Heaven. Henry was not a faithful attendant at services. But he was a good man, a charitable one. He did not neglect his tithing, and if the Gilbert pew was often empty, it is quite understandable, because he had been plagued by illness for many years."

He touched her hand lightly, briefly, his fingertips as soft as a butterfly's wings. "You must not grieve, my dear. He has gone to his just reward."

She stiffened herself against a feeling of sympathy for a kindly old man who could not find his life in Holy Orders very easy these days. She did not care for the prospect of disturbing the serenity of his unworldly existence. But she had to ask the question, and she spoke loudly so that she would not have to repeat it.

"Are you sure that it is my grandfather who's in the grave?"

His eyes flew open wide, sending his sparse white eyebrows soaring. His prayerbook slipped from his fingers and struck the ground with a light thud. Rosemary stepped forward to pick it up, but he scooped it up with a surprisingly spry motion.

The exertion had put color into his face. He drew a few gasping breaths and then stuttered, "My dear young lady! I don't know what you mean!" And then, with a softening of his features, he said in a mild, uninflected voice, "Oh, I see how it is, my dear! You have not been able to accept the fact that he is dead. Yes, I have found this to be true in many cases. The bereaved cling to the idea that their loved one could not have left them. You were very fond of him, I assume."

Even the effort of speaking seemed to exhaust him. But when Rosemary put her mouth close to his ear and said, "I thought I saw him at Fairview last night . . ." he told her.

"People sometimes have these so-called visions, too. Especially soon after death. I can assure you, if it will bring you comfort, that Henry Gilbert has indeed passed on. I knew him for many years, and I saw his face before the coffin was closed."

Then, evidently seeing the look of hopeless bewilderment on her face, he said, "Perhaps you would like to come into the church and pray, my child. You would be very welcome."

She shook her head and muttered something about the tide, which would be at its highest point in a little while, and not getting through the road. She left him there among his dead parishioners, a wistful expression on his old face because not enough people were interested in praying in this modern, confusing world.

Chapter Six

DREW'S CAR was in the driveway when Rosemary came up it. He had a hose in his hand and was spraying water on the hood. By the time she drew up behind him, he had gone to the faucet on the side of the house and turned off the hose.

When he signalled her to roll down her window, she shook her head. She did not want to speak to Drew at this moment. She had not been able, on the way back from Grist Mill Corners, to think about anything but keeping the car on that narrow, windy road. She wanted to be alone now and think about what she had seen and heard, and to try to make sense out of it.

So she ignored Drew's handwaving and sat waiting for him to drive off and give her access to the coach house. He came striding to the car and yanked open the door, glaring.

"You ungrateful brat! I was going to tell you to leave this hunk here and that I'd wash it, too. Now you can do it yourself!"

It was so much like one of their childish quarrels that she could not help laughing. Drew stood there with a shamefaced grin, looking much like he had when, in his early teens, he had been given a severe reprimand.

"Oh, Drew!" Rosemary gasped. "Are we going to have this hassle every time I have to park my car?"

He put out his hand to help her out. "Very likely. We never did get along very well, did we? And under this deceptively manly and handsome exterior beats a heart of pure venom. So get your weapons ready, girl!"

His hand was still on her arm. They were facing each

40

other now, her chin lifted and his eyes looking down into hers. In a sudden movement, he pulled her against him. His free hand fastened around the back of her neck, and his mouth came down and covered hers.

She stood very still, her own arms hanging limp as the kiss grew stronger, robbing her of her breath, sending all her senses into a dizzying whirl.

When finally the mindless spinning stopped, she raised her arms and broke out of the circle of his and pushed him away.

There was nothing she could do about her voice at that moment. Her throat was becoming constricted, and her protest was a thin and uneven squeak.

"Drew! What in Heaven's name was that for? You shouldn't have—"

"I missed it yesterday, remember? After all these years . . . old friends when they meet again." He, too, seemed to be having trouble speaking, in spite of the nonchalant words. "Nothing to put on a three-act drama about, was it?"

"It was a silly thing to do, that's all."

She rubbed a hand over her mouth, as though she could scrub away the memory of that crazy moment when the world had seemed to tilt and spin. The gesture evidently angered him, because his features hardened and he said harshly, "You don't have to worry about it becoming hab-it-forming."

For a few more minutes she remained there, gazing into his clenched face. In spite of the fact that she had often been hurt by his teasing when they were children together, and even though the thing that had sprung up between them had been disturbing and regrettable, she wished that she could talk frankly to Drew.

He had been her friend. She had looked up to him and been grateful to him when he deigned to let her tag along behind him. And now she needed a friend. Drew had been her oracle, the source of all wisdom when she was seven and eight and nine. She wanted to tell him that she had seen her grandfather, as alive as he had ever been during those summers of long ago.

She was tempted to blurt out the rest of it, too: that she knew there was someone occupying the second floor ell, that there was someone else in Farview besides Edith and her and the two Swift women and Drew.

But her nerves still felt a little stretched and her emotions were too close to the surface. If he laughed at her . . . But of course he would laugh. She could almost hear him hooting.

"You nitwit!" he would say. "You imbecilic brat!" That had been his much-used putdown. She was not going to give him a chance to use it now.

He put out his hand, and she shrank back. A great roar of laughter came from somewhere in his chest and when it died away, he said, "Good Lord, child, did you think I had evil designs on you? All I want is your keys. Give them to me, and I'll put your car away again."

They made a jangling noise as he tossed them into the air and then caught them again. His eyes probed her face for a silent moment.

"There's something else, isn't there?" he asked. "You're not uptight just because I kissed you. Are you going to tell me that it's never happened before with all those countless swains you must have had, a girl as pretty as you?"

His jeering sounded weak. She thought she could detect a note of kindness in his voice, and his eyes had darkened and looked sober. She fought down the temptation to tell him where she had been and why. She did not want to be laughed at again.

"Hundreds of times," she said, smiling sunnily at him. "I can't remember all their names. There were several— although I can't recall much about them, either—who ended up in mental institutions, made mad by my beauty."

She thought she had acquitted herself fairly well. She could not hear so much as a chuckle as she turned on her heel, crossed the driveway, and went hastily up the steps.

Bertha Swift—Rosemary had found a way to distinguish between the two hired girls: Bertha had a faint red birthmark high on her neck—was coming out of the kitchen and stopped when she saw Rosemary. She beckoned and said in a low voice, "Mrs. Chester wants me to tell you that your dinner will be served in your room tonight. She's lying down, not feeling as pert as she might. So since there'll just be you—Mr. Chester eating his meals some- wheres else most of the time—she said it would be easier on us were you to be taken up a tray."

Rosemary failed to see the logic in that. It would be less work for Bertha to serve her something at the kitchen table than to have to arrange a tray and carry it upstairs. Years ago, Rosemary had often had snacks and full course meals in the kitchen. Usually it had happened when she had been so engrossed in play that she had forgotten the time, or during the crowded weekends at Farview when Edith's guests had been entertained with a sit-down din- ner.

She could not quite bring herself to say that aloud. There was something forbidding about this stiff-mannered New England woman. Rosemary thought back, trying again to place Bertha in the memories of her childhood summers; she could not. When she sat at the kitchen table, sometimes with Drew, it had been a fiercely independent Mrs. Somebody—she could not recall the name—who had scolded and complained in the same sort of twangy voice.

"Drew? He doesn't eat here at all?"

Rosemary did not expect an answer, at least not a forthright one. She anticipated that Bertha would say that it was none of her business what he did and hint that it wasn't any of Rosemary's, either. She was surprised that there was any response at all, and almost shocked by the woman's frankness.

"Breakfasts, sometimes. He's got other interests." The titter that came through those severe lips was the most surprising thing of all. "Moonstruck, that's what's ailing him. He's over to the Corners day and night."

Rosemary knew well enough what the woman meant, but she wanted to hear it said in simpler terms. So that there would be no mistake.

She asked bluntly, "Drew has a—a girl friend here? He's seriously interested in someone? Romantically?"

"You could say that." The heavy coil of hair atop Bertha's head slid forward as she nodded. She put her hand up to it, drew out a long, wicked-looking hairpin, and fastened it tightly again. "Over to the Corners. He's courting her."

As she went upstairs, Rosemary told herself that the reason for Drew's being in Farview should not have surprised her. And it cleared up one of the things she had been wondering about. He had fallen in love with a girl from the village, probably last summer, and not being able to stay away from her, had come back to persuade her to marry him.

It was a simple explanation, not at all difficult to understand. And none of her business, she thought. Then why the twitching of anger? And why the lagging of her footsteps and the blindness to the things around her?

Neither she nor Drew had ever had anything to do with the village people when they were youngsters. The penny candy store and the few excursions down to the public bathing beach were all they had known of Grist Mill Corners. She could not remember ever having been inside Father Lyman's Episcopal church or eating in any of the restaurants that were open during the warm months.

Edith had spoken carelessly and condescendingly of the year-round residents, and none of them had been invited to her parties. Then why and how had Drew—?

Rosemary went into her room and banged the door behind her, as though she could shut out the agitation that had, she kept trying to tell herself, no cause at all.

What was Drew to her? How could it matter that he was here in this bleak place, at this raw, miserable time of the year, because he was in love with one of the local belles?

That was the ultimate of snobbery, and Rosemary regretted the snide thought before it was scarcely formed. She tried to put out of her mind Drew and his summer romance which had developed into something serious.

She had seen him only twice since she had been here in Farview, and both times they had come close to quarreling. But there had been one heart-shaking moment when he had taken her into his arms and pressed his lips on hers, and she had been lost in a warm and wonderful spell.

So he had kissed her. So he was a two-timer, a heel, a wolf. Rosemary pulled out of her memory all the old slang words she had ever heard that were appropriate for describing him.

But perhaps it had been as he said: the kiss might have been a form of greeting—started that way, at least, and then got out of hand. There would be no others, she vowed grimly. Drew, in love with one girl, was not going to be allowed to play dangerous little games with another.

Rosemary sat down on the faded pink slipper chair and tried to interest herself in one of the books she had brought upstairs the night before. She read only the first chapter—enough to learn that Annabella was in love with Derek, who was affianced to Pamela, who loved the dark and mysterious Lord Lenstone, who lusted after Annabella.

But she could not focus her attention on what came next, and the prospect of reading three hundred pages more to learn who the seemingly witless heroine would end up marrying did not excite her.

It was growing dark when Lucinda Swift brought Rosemary's supper. She did not linger, merely told Rosemary to leave the tray and the dishes outside her door when she had finished eating. There was haste in her movements, and her footsteps were quick as she went down the corridor in the direction of the ell.

Rosemary strained her ears to hear any sounds coming from that shut-off part of the house. There were none. But the feeling that Farview held some other sort of life beneath its surface came back and possessed her mind stubbornly.

Her supper finished, Rosemary was left again with Annabella and all her romantic complications. She had read only a few more pages when the print began to melt and squirm in her vision. She yawned twice, and her eyes became flooded with tears. The book slipped from her hands, but she was suddenly too tired to lean over and pick it up. Her head fell against the back of the chair as a great wave of darkness swallowed her up in sleep.

* * *

When she awoke, there was a band of dim, watery moonlight across her bed. The rectangle of windowpane under its shade gleamed faintly. Rosemary, all her muscles cramped and aching, pulled herself out of her chair and went to the window. She had intended to lower the shade so that the light would not keep her awake when she got into bed. But when she touched it, it was like some living thing in her hand. It sprang upward and rolled itself around its holder with a sharp little sound that was loud in the stillness.

When her startled heart resumed its normal beating, Rosemary reached for a chair, intending to climb up on it to retrieve the shade and pull it down. But her legs felt weak and shaky, and there was a strange numbness in her body that went beyond the lethargy of the first moments of awakening.

She let her head fall against the cool expanse of the windowpane and tried to focus her eyes, which felt hot and heavy, by looking down at the grounds.

And then she saw it. The body of a man, hanging from a thick branch of an oak tree, swung lightly in the late-night wind.

Chapter Seven

She could neither move nor cry out for a single, heart-stopping moment. Then the blood began to run through her veins in a freezing flood. Her voice became unlocked, and as she backed away from the window, she screamed.

Turning, she raced across the room and yanked open the door leading to the hall. When she screamed again, the sound echoed along the corridor. She was suddenly too weak to go another step. She clung to the door jamb until her fingers, growing nerveless, slid down the expanse of wood and threw her off balance.

She felt her knees sinking toward the floor, her head swimming, and the burning sensation in her eyes blotting out everything in front of her. She could barely turn her head when she heard the creaking of a door, faint and seeming to come from a long way behind her.

When she had pulled herself upright with what little strength she could manage, she saw a tall figure silhouetted against the feeble light coming through the open door which led to the ell.

Then, with a little sigh, she released her hold on the jamb, and a swirling cloud of blackness enveloped her as she sank down upon the floor.

What happened next was as unreal as a vague dream. Rosemary felt herself being lifted up by strong arms, carried into her bedroom and placed carefully onto the bed. Then the blackness grew deeper and thicker until it smothered all feeling and all awareness.

The morning was almost gone when she awakened. Her memory came back immediately, and with it, sharply outlined pictures in all their horror. Her senses had never been stronger. The sound of the surf was like background music for a replay of what she had seen and heard during the night.

She threw back the bedclothes and ran to the window. After the rain of the past few days, everything on the grounds looked fresh and clean. Trees and grass and bushes sparkled in the sunlight. There was only an instant when her mind touched on the grass and the shrubbery. She was staring at a lower branch of the twisted oak tree, which towered almost as tall as the house.

No body hung suspended from it.

She put her fingers on her eyeballs and rubbed them gently, as though she could force out of her vision what she saw below her window now and replace it with what she had seen during the dark hours. When she looked again, everything was exactly the same: the branches moving in the wind, the sun burnishing the bushes, dead leaves of another season wet and slimy on the narrow path in what had once been a garden.

And there was no body hanging from the tree.

Rosemary bathed, combed her hair, put on her makeup and slacks and a heavy sweater, doing all those things in a mechanical sort of way because her mind was engaged with other things. When she went downstairs, she could hear voices coming from the kitchen, the rattling of dishes, and the clattering of pans. They were normal, cheerful sounds, not those of a house where a death had taken place less than a dozen hours before.

When she went into the kitchen, a conversation that had been in progress between Bertha Swift and her sister broke off abruptly. There were still traces of liveliness in their faces for a moment before they changed their expressions into polite, inquiring ones.

"I'm looking for my aunt," Rosemary said in a voice that quavered a little. "I overslept. I suppose she has already had breakfast."

Bertha looked significantly at the clock over the stove. "It'll be time for lunch soon. Unless you want a cup of coffee?"

Rosemary shook her head. "I must see Mrs. Chester. Have you any idea where she is?"

"Went for a walk, so she said. An hour ago, that was. Should be back soon."

It was Lucinda who had spoken. In spite of the fact that she had not said anything out of the ordinary, Rosemary thought she detected something that did not quite ring true. When Lucinda and Bertha had been talking together earlier as she was coming along the first floor hall, Rosemary had heard warmth and richness in their voices. The unmistakable, and almost exaggerated, twang had been gone.

She did not have time to puzzle over that now. She had to find Edith as quickly as possible. And although the two women were half smiling at her and obviously trying to be helpful, Rosemary had the uneasy feeling that she was not welcome in their kitchen. The smiles did not reach their eyes, which were as cold and pale as ice.

She mumbled "Thanks," went back down the hall to the front door, and opened it. In spite of the bright sunlight, there was a chill in the air, and her sweater was not quite warm enough for a windy March day. She was about to go back to her room for her coat when she saw Edith come jogging up the driveway.

The woman wore a heavy woolen garment that made her body look bulky. There were sneakers on her feet and a silk kerchief over her hair, but in spite of the unbecoming costume she looked strikingly beautiful. The wind and the exercise had brought a rosy glow to her skin, and her eyes were brilliant. She looked girlish and carefree, and when Rosemary ran forward to meet her, she stopped, laughing and panting.

"You must do this with me some morning," she gasped. "When you feel stronger, of course. It's hard work, but fun, darling!"

They were standing directly under the tree from which Rosemary had seen dangling the body of a man. Yet all that she was able to say was, "Bertha said you'd gone out for a walk."

"I jog every morning when the weather is good." There was a note of pride in Edith's voice which turned to concern. "Were you worried about me, dear? They could have told you where I was. They've seen me in this hundreds of times." She lifted her arms and looked down ruefully at her suit. "Stupid girls! But they've been here forever, so I have to make allowances for them. You are upset, aren't you, sweetie?"

Rosemary did not answer at once. She was thinking that neither Bertha nor Lucinda appeared to be in the least stupid and that they had not been employed in Farview "forever," because thirteen years ago there had been a different staff of servants.

Her thoughts returned to Edith, who was saying, "I thought you must be having a good long sleep. We didn't hear a peep from you all morning. I told them you weren't to be disturbed, that you needed your rest. You did sleep well, didn't you, darling?" she asked anxiously. "No more nightmares?"

If she had been trying deliberately, she could not have made more difficult what Rosemary had to say. The girl's voice was thin and unsteady when she blurted, "Aunt Edith, who was the man who died here last night?" She raised a hand and pointed at the branch above her head. "He was hanging there, a rope around his neck, his head lolling. I didn't see much of his face, just a glimpse because it was—it was too horrible! It did look sort of familiar, although I didn't really recognize it."

Her mind was groping backward. The face she now felt she had seen somewhere before, the slender body, the somewhat out-of-date suit—she struggled to remember all the things she had seen in that dreadful moonlit scene.

"I did see him, Aunt Edith! I did!"

Edith had neither moved nor attempted to say a word while her niece was speaking. When her absorption with that awful moment at her window loosened its hold, Rosemary saw the thinned mouth, the stricken expression in the lovely eyes.

"It was right there, hanging from that branch." Rosemary's voice began to peter away. "You must believe me!"

Edith put out a hand and clasped it over Rosemary's. "My poor child," she crooned. "You *have* been having a bad time! I'm afraid whatever medicine it is you're taking . . ."

"Vitamins, that's all!"

And then the suspicion that had been nibbling at one corner of her mind, so far without form or definition, rose and took shape.

"I don't take anything, not sleeping pills or drugs of any sort! But last night—last night, something I ate or drank must have affected me in some way. Because I fell deeply asleep—well, passed out is what it was like. I barely made the bed. And when I came to, I went to the window and saw it. What I told you about. So if there was any sort of drug that I took, it was not of my own choosing."

Edith had stiffened. Her eyes had kindled with an angry, incredulous light.

She said, in a tone that was steely, "Are you trying to tell me that someone in this house deliberately drugged you, Rosemary? You expect me to believe that? You come to me with stories about seeing my father still alive in his bed, although he has been dead for more than two weeks. And then this weird story of a man hanging from a tree on the grounds." Her expression softened. "Darling, we must find you a doctor. Unfortunately, there are none of the right kind at the Corners. No matter. I shall drive you into Portland, if necessary, and find one there."

"I suppose you're talking about a psychiatrist," Rosemary said testily. "Aunt Edith, I assure you that I don't need one. I am not mentally disturbed or in need of therapy or anything like that."

The woman laughed lightly. "My dear, silly child! I'd never have expected you to have that old-fashioned attitude. I was in analysis for some months when I was in New York. Practically everyone I knew was, too. You must let us help you, sweetie. I don't want your visit here completely ruined by these dreadful nightmares. You've been here only two nights and during both of them, you've heard and seen things that never could have been real."

"I haven't told you all of it," Rosemary persisted, stubbornness hardening inside her. "Last night, when I saw what I told you I did, I screamed. I'm surprised that none of you heard that. I ran out of my room wanting, I guess, to find someone to cut down that—that horrible thing. And when I got as far as the hall, a man came out of the ell. The one in my part of the hall, Aunt Edith; the one you told me no one must go into because it's dangerous."

Edith asked quietly, "A man? What man? Who was he?"

"I have no idea." Rosemary's mind went groping backward again. The face, seen only briefly in that moment before she had fainted, was like a blurred picture. "He looked like—well, he looked familiar; but it couldn't be him. At any rate, he carried me back into my room."

"That's quite a story." Edith's laugh tinkled faintly. "Another of your strange dreams, I'm afraid. The ell has

been shut off for months. There could not have been a
man in it. No, darling, there couldn't have been anyone
like that. You were mistaken."

Chapter Eight

ROSEMARY SAID, a rough shading of anger in her voice, "I
will not be spoken to as a child, Aunt Edith. I can't believe that you can go on lying this way! You told me that
the ell on my side of the hall is so in need of repair that it
could be dangerous. And yet it wasn't only that man I saw
last night."

The name very nearly came to her lips and then slipped
away again. She knew him, or she had seen his picture
somewhere. But when her mind came close to capturing
the elusive thought, it fluttered away.

"Not only him," she said staunchly in the face of
Edith's indulgent smile. "I saw Bertha coming out of that
place, through the door at the end of the hall, and I
know . . ."

What she knew was not to be divulged, because Edith
moved around her and broke into a trot. The wind swept
her voice away as she ran toward the house. All that
Rosemary heard was something about "get out of this
foolish suit."

She watched the woman disappear through the front
door, then turned away slowly and started down the driveway. There was a rustic bench between the trees halfway
down the slight slope. The small imitation logs that
formed its seat looked damp, and they were not, she found
when she sat on them, in the least comfortable. But it was
quiet there, as quiet as it ever could be within the sound of
the surf. And it was peaceful beyond the shadow of the big

house, which was almost hidden from view by the gnarled old trees.

But her thoughts were far from tranquil, because she had seen a dead man hanging from the branch of one of those trees. The night of her arrival at Farview, she had seen someone who was buried in the churchyard in the village. She was almost certain that someone had drugged her and that she might just possibly have been hallucinating.

There was the other man, the one she had seen silhouetted in the doorway of the ell. He had lifted her into his arms and carried her into her room and placed her on her bed. She had felt the strength of his arms and smelled his shaving lotion. She could remember that scent, and ghosts and imaginary figures were, she supposed, without odor. He had been real. She tried to recall what he looked like. Only a glimpse, but she could remember the long, pale face and the gray-flecked hair and his easiness and grace of movement. He had worn some sort of sandals, which were noiseless on the thin carpet of the second floor hall.

Rosemary shut her eyes and could see him. His face was imprinted on her mind, but not only because she had seen it that once: there had been something else, something she read in the newspaper a few weeks ago. There had been a picture with the story.

She remembered the name now. It was Martin Morse.

It was too fantastic to be believed! She rejected the thought, jeering at herself for imagining, even for a moment, that she had seen the man who was reputed to be worth billions of dollars in a shadowy corridor in Farview last night.

She went on sitting there, staring down the driveway but seeing nothing. What she knew about Martin Morse's life and background unreeled through her mind.

He was in his early forties. He had been a noted sportsman, a scuba diver, polo player, airplane pilot, sky diver, and all his activities had been written up in the newspapers and in magazines to the point of satiation. Within the short time since he had disappeared, two or three versions

of his biography had been written and published in paper-
back form.

Rosemary remembered that his romances, too, had
filled columns of newsprint through the years. He had
been rumored engaged to be married a dozen times:
movie actresses, heiresses, noted beauties—his name had
been coupled with a vast army of them. Although he had
always been publicity shy, photographers in New York
and Hollywood and the fashionable places of Europe had
snapped his pictures with one lovely and exciting young
woman after another.

At some time—within the past few years, Rosemary
thought—he had become a recluse. These things she knew
only vaguely, because she had never been much interested
in Martin Morse or any of the so-called beautiful people
who flitted from continent to continent in search of pleas-
ure. That way of life was so different from her own that it
seemed unreal, a tinsel sort of world about which she read
while she was under a dryer in a beauty shop.

Martin Morse could not have come out of the ell and
carried her back to her bed. Perhaps she had dreamed the
whole thing, as Edith claimed. For if Rosemary's screaming had been loud enough to be heard in that closed-off
part of the house, why had not Edith or Drew or one of
the hired girls come in answer to it?

All the bizarre things that had happened to her since
she had come to Farview spun through her mind: seeing
Henry Gilbert alive, when there could be no doubt about
his being dead and buried; the appearance of a man who
could not possibly be Martin Morse, although he was as
much like him as an identical twin; seeing the body hanging from a branch of the oak tree.

That face, dropped forward and pale in the moonlight,
that corpse face suspended and with a rope around its
neck, swam into her memory.

It must be my day for remembering, she thought wryly.
Or seeing resemblances where none exist, because that
young man's features were those she had seen in pictures
accompanying newspaper stories a few years ago.

With a great deal of difficulty, identification like a tatter

of mist coming close to the edge of her mind and then flut-
tering away, she captured it finally, was able to match the
face with a name.

Roland Harmon.

It came back in a rush, the story of the kidnapping of a
wealthy young man five years ago. Rosemary had been
seventeen then, at her most sensitive and impressionable
age. She remembered how the story of a boy her own age
being snatched away from his parents' home had moved
her sympathies. He had never, as far as she knew, been
seen again.

He was one of those missing persons she had read about
in the news account of Martin Morse's disappearance.
There had been no picture with the story, but in her mind
she saw the boyish, slightly drooping mouth, the lock of
hair tumbling over a smooth brow, the delicate nose and
uneven eyebrows.

But that could not have been so, either. Roland Harmon and Martin Morse, both of whom she had read about
in that newspaper story, could not have been here in Farview. Edith Chester had been right. What Rosemary
thought she had seen had been a particularly vivid dream.
Thoughts of the two men—and Henry Gilbert, too—had
imbedded themselves in her subconscious mind and come
out in the form of a nightmare, which she had imagined to
be real.

Rosemary started when she heard someone speak her
name. So engrossed had she been in her thoughts that she
did not hear the sound of footsteps coming along the
driveway, did not know that she was not alone on the
grounds until Drew said, "Rosemary!" Then she saw his
shadow, which fell across her and blotted out the sun.

"Cold day," he said easily. "What are you doing out
here?"

She blinked up at him and cleared the confusion out of
her brain. She did not know how much of what she had
been thinking to tell him. If he laughed at her—and of
course he would laugh—there might be another sharp
quarrel, and she felt too upset and agitated to hold up her
end in an exchange of words.

"Just getting a little fresh air," she told him. "There doesn't seem much of anything else to do around here. What do you find to do?"

She was deliberately giving him an opening to confide in her. She did not actually expect him to explain about the girl who lived in the village and his reason for being in this gloomy place at this time of the year. And he did not.

He sat down beside her and said easily, "Follow you around."

"For what reason?"

"Can't you guess?" he asked. "Because I've fallen wildly, madly in love with you. I'm trailing you, waiting for the right moment to lay my heart at your feet."

"Drew, don't!"

He turned at the sound of distress in her voice. "What's up, dear? You look—oh, heck, I don't know! Like you've been seeing spooks or something. Come on, tell Uncle Drew all your troubles." His arm slid around the back of the bench, and she pulled away from it and sat up straighter.

"I just don't feel in the mood for that sort of rubbish." Then she burst out pettishly, "You should be saving that sort of talk for your girlfriend."

She slid a glance at his face and saw on it an expression that looked like genuine bewilderment.

"How's that again? What girl?"

So he was going to lie about it and was going to continue the silly game if she permitted it.

"Forget I said it, Drew. It's none of my business anyway. You can have a dozen local sweethearts, and it wouldn't concern me in the least. I wish you'd go away and leave me alone."

Her voice betrayed her by breaking in what sounded very much like a sob. She drew away to the end of the bench with her face turned in the other direction. She did not look at him until he edged closer. He put his hand on her cheek and forced her to face him.

"Rosemary!" He sounded grave and concerned, and his eyes were sober. "We didn't get along all that well when we were kids, but we should be able to do better now. And we never lied to each other or kept private secrets. It's true, I *have* been following you around, but it's because— well, because there's something that I can't talk about right now."

"In other words," she choked, "it's a one-sided deal. I'm supposed to confide in you, but you keep your secrets to yourself. And tell me untruths. And talk in that silly way."

She was trembling, and in spite of her good intentions, she was not remaining calm but was being swept up into a quarrel that seemed oddly out of balance. Because the man who was reaching for her hands did not look in the least perturbed. There seemed to be a hard glitter far back in his eyes, but it did not appear to be the shine of anger. She snatched her hands away and knotted them together.

"I wish," she said coldly, "that you would leave me alone!"

"As you like, madame!" He jumped to his feet, swept an imaginary hat from his head, and made a deep bow. "I will return to my car, which, I hope, appreciates me more than you do."

Then, before he turned and left her, he said soberly, "I'll be in the garage doing a little work on the engine, in case you need me."

She sat there a little longer while the wind snatched tendrils of hair from under her kerchief and the cold air bit at her feet and fingers and stained her face with color. The sea was noisy. She remembered a little sheltered spot, almost entirely enclosed by a formation of bushes, at the edge of the cliff where she used to sit and watch the tide come in when she was a child. She had always loved the ocean—still a novelty to a little girl from the Midwest— and since her arrival at Farview, she'd had no more than a few brief glimpses of it.

Perhaps the sight of it now would chase away the lingering anger at Drew, about whom she did not want to think, and would let her forget, for a time at least, her strange fancies about all she believed she had seen and heard in the house that loomed behind her.

She started toward the cliff, feeling her feet sink into the spongy grass of the lawn. But she did not reach it.

For she did not see the hole that lay in her path until it was too late, an oblong-shaped hole as long and wide and deep as a grave. Her arms went up from her sides as she tried to hold her balance. She felt her heels sliding downward and her fingers curled in a clutching motion, but there was nothing to grasp. And as she slipped into that deep hole, she brought an avalanche of dirt with her, a swift flow of earth that continued even after she fell, face downward, against the bottom of the pit.

The dirt was covering her feet and legs and the motion of its falling had loosened the soil on the other side of the hole. In spite of being slightly stunned by the fall, she realized with horror that she would soon be completely buried. Literally buried alive.

Chapter Nine

SHE TRIED to struggle to her feet, but the soft ground defeated her and she fell against it, felt it in her nose and eyes and against her mouth. She raised herself on her hands, dug her heels into the dirt, and lifted her body to a squatting position.

The slide of soil was diminishing gradually, but when she finally drew up erect, she saw that she was imprisoned. The lawn was at least two feet over her head, and there was no way that she could reach it; if she tried to climb that soft surface, she would start another avalanche of dirt.

She drew a deep breath and began to scream. Then she waited, her heart pumping heavily, to learn if she had been heard. Not in the house; she did not expect that. But

Drew had said he would be in the garage working on his car. He was her only hope. If he did not hear her, she would go on being trapped in this dreadful hole until she was too weak to cry out.

Wrapping her sweater around her more tightly, she tried to free herself of the cold shivering which was spreading through her entire body. The chattering of her teeth made it difficult for her to scream again. Even to her own ears, the shriek sounded weak. But she repeated it again and again, until the screaming turned to sobbing and she had no strength left to do anything except lean against the soft wall of the pit and let the dirt mingle with her tears.

The terror was like a form of physical illness that robbed her of all other feeling. Her brain felt numb, and she thought vaguely of insanity, wondered if she would become mad here in this awful prison before Death came to release her.

She was on the edge of insanity now, she was certain; imagining things like footsteps on the damp lawn and a voice saying her name, the footsteps stopping and the voice growing louder.

But when she looked up, there was a face peering down into the hole. It hung there, white and oval like a cutout cardboard mask, only the eyes alive and dark with disbelief.

She did not recognize it in that first unseeing glance when she stood, her feet almost covered by the thick, wet earth and her head hanging back at an uncomfortable angle, and looked upward. Her mind, befogged by the horror, came slowly back to awareness. She was not sure even then that it was Drew on the lawn above her. She had been screaming for him with such fervor that she was not sure whether it was he or a figment of her imagination.

When he spoke, she knew that this was real, not a fancy. He called down, "What in the name of all that's holy are you doing down there, Rosie?"

It was so typically Drew that a choke of laughter almost strangled her. She could feel the rising hysteria shuddering inside her, and she threw her arms around her body as though to protect herself from it.

"What do you think I'm doing?" she chattered. "Waiting for a bus? I fell, you idiot! I was lucky I didn't break an arm or a leg, or smother to death."

The good, healthy surge of anger cleared her brain. She said waspishly, "Well, don't just stand there! Do something about getting me out of here."

Drew bent forward and held out a hand. She could not even reach it, and she shook her head impatiently at him. "Not that way. I can't climb up the side. The dirt is too soft. Get a ladder. There must be one around somewhere."

His face disappeared, and she heard the sound of his footsteps above her head. It seemed, as she stood there cold and uncomfortable with the wet grime drying on her face and hands and clothing, that he was gone for a long time. But he finally came back with a ladder and lowered it down carefully. She pulled her feet out of the muddy earth and climbed up with slow and cautious steps.

He put out his hand and helped her onto the lawn. They looked at each other silently for a long moment. She did not know what to say to him, how to thank him, tell him how grateful she was. She was trying to choose the words when he said, "Good Lord, what a mess you are!"

She glared at him bitterly. "Thanks a lot! I haven't just come from a beauty shop, you know. I might have expected something like that from you!"

He was grinning, and she realized that he had deliberately tried to rouse her to anger, and was pleased that he had succeeded. Probably, she thought, he had been afraid that she would throw herself on his chest and weep and wail. There were tears; they began to drench her eyes and spill down her cheeks. She rubbed at them with the palms of her hands, grinding the dirt into her skin, until Drew clasped his fingers over her wrists and pulled her hands away.

"Crying's not going to help anything," he said. "Try a hot shower and a lot of soap."

That was not what she wanted at that moment. There

were questions clamoring in her brain, and she wanted them answered before she left him.

"Who dug that hole? And in that particular place? Anyone crossing the lawn at this point would be certain to fall in and maybe suffer some sort of serious injury."

"Anyone else," Drew growled, "would look where she was going."

"Not necessarily. I was looking out toward the ocean. The whitecaps were high. It would be only natural for somebody walking toward the cliff to be watching them. I don't think any of the others in the house would be going in that direction. Aunt Edith was out jogging a little while ago. She's had enough exercise, I would imagine, for today. The two women, the Swifts, are probably still busy in the kitchen. So I would be the only one—"

His grip on her wrists tightened and he said roughly, "Hey, wait a minute! Are you trying to tell me that you think someone deliberately dug that hole on the chance that you'd fall into it? Oh, come on! What would be the sense in that?"

"I don't know. I don't know anything about anything. Not why I saw my grandfather alive, although he's supposed to be dead, or why that man was hanging from the tree, or what Martin Morse is doing in the house. All those things—is it so strange for me to believe that someone wants me dead?"

He stood looking at her for such a long time that she began to have the strange feeling she was in some sort of spell that had turned her body cold and hard and stone-like. She saw him as a stranger, someone she had met only a few minutes ago. He was standing with his back to the sun, and his face, in shadow, looked dark and unfamiliar.

He pulled his hands away and let them drop to his side. When he spoke again his voice, although quiet, sounded strained.

"I have no idea what any of that means. It's a lot of mishmash. You want to postpone getting cleaned up long enough to tell me the answers to those riddles?"

She wanted, suddenly, only to be away from him. A hideous thought had snaked its way into her mind. Drew was the only person in Farview who could have dug that hole. Only he would have been able to take a shovel from the tools in the cellar, come out here on the grounds, and work, unnoticed, to make a grave.

When had he done so? Last night, when the others in the house were asleep? Or early this morning, before anyone else was awake?

If Edith or one of the servant girls had noticed what he was doing, he could have said that he was digging up the lawn for planting purposes. But he had taken a chance. If he was observed digging deeply into the earth, he could have had no explanation.

Rosemary's thoughts broke off abruptly. If Drew had made a deliberate effort to do her harm, wouldn't he have left her there in the pit to go on screaming until she had no breath left and collapsed in weakness and despair?

She did not know what to think. Her mind raced, first in one direction and then in another. The man standing in front of her was a fiend who had attempted to murder her and then, a moment later, her rescuer and old friend. She tried to remember what he had said about a legacy from her grandfather when she first arrived at Farview. He had hinted that she'd had an ulterior motive in coming back to Farview.

"You thought that part of this was going to fall into your hot little hands?"

She could remember the words, but not the tone he had used. She did not know, at this moment, whether he had been teasing her, as he had often done when they were children, or whether he had been voicing resentment.

There had been no notification of any kind from anybody that she was to share in her grandfather's fortune. She was vague about such things, but she guessed that the estate had not yet been settled. And if she died, in a way that was meant to seem accidental, who would benefit from her death? Edith? And Drew, if he was a participant in a plot to put Rosemary out of the way?

She was appalled by the things she was thinking. She could not go on looking at him for fear he could read the vile thoughts that were confusing her and making her feel a little ill.

"Later," she said, forcing her voice to sound even. "I've got to get out of these filthy things. We'll talk later."

She did not look back as she walked away, but she sensed that he was standing there, his eyes on her back. She went up the steps to the porch with a steady and unhurried tread, but when she reached the front hall, she broke into a run. She did not want to meet anyone, looking the way she did. She did not want to bring back the horror by having to explain what had happened to her.

When she had finished her bath and shampoo and changed into clean clothing, she went down to luncheon. Edith was there in the breakfast room, as poised and easy mannered as always. Her lovely voice had in it the familiar music.

"Well, darling, are you managing to amuse yourself? I was afraid it might be boring here for you."

Then why, Rosemary asked silently, did you urge me to come?

"But there's Drew, and you must be able to find things to do together."

When all he wants is to spend all his time with some girl in the village? Rosemary could not hold that back.

"He's in love, isn't he? With someone he hopes to marry? That's the reason he's here now, right?"

Edith looked uncomfortable. "I'm sure it's nothing but a passing fancy. He'd never be serious about her, not to the point of marriage. Drew has had dozens of girls since he was old enough to date. But the romantic flurries never lasted long. Darling, I'm afraid my stepson is—well, it's an old-fashioned word, and your generation doesn't use it anymore—a philanderer."

Her face brightened with a smile. "He never forgot you, dear. He's often spoken of you. When you were here before, he was—what? Thirteen? Fourteen? I think that perhaps you were his first love."

Rosemary's mouth fell open in astonishment. When she could speak again, she cried, "But that's crazy! I was nine the last time I saw him. And he used to torment me and do everything he could to make my life miserable. Aunt Edith, that's probably the most foolish thing anyone ever said to me!"

"Little boys are like that, you know they are." Edith let her voice linger over a bell-like laugh. "That's the only way, at that age, they can show a special feeling for a girl. I had hoped. . . ." She let the words drift away on a sigh.

The last part of what she said did not make any impression on Rosemary at first. The picture of Drew as a teenager smitten with puppy love for her nine-year-old self was so ludicrous that she could feel the laughter bubbling inside her, and she had to struggle to keep a straight face as she looked across the table at Edith. Then the significance of the woman's unfinished sentence struck her. She realized that what Edith had said, her use of the word "hoped," had a meaning which she found abhorrent. The feeling grew stronger as her aunt dropped her head forward a little and peered at her through long, thick eyelashes. She was waiting for Rosemary to confide in her, to say that it was because of Drew that she had come back to the vacation place of her childhood.

It was not true, of course. And if Edith had invited her here to divert Drew from one of his little romantic interludes, she was going to be vastly disappointed.

This thing with the girl in the village must be more serious than any of his love affairs thus far—so serious, in fact, that Edith had felt impelled to throw Rosemary and Drew together in the hope that what she imagined they had shared as children would be rekindled.

It *was* ridiculous, and Rosemary was about to say so aloud. But Edith had finished her luncheon, replaced her cup on its saucer, and pushed back her chair.

"I'm going into the village this afternoon. Do you want to drive in with me, or would you rather stay home and rest? The girls—Bertha and Lucinda—are going with me. This is their afternoon off."

Rosemary opted for the nap. Lunch had been too heavy: a shrimp and noodle casserole, hot rolls, broccoli, and creamy tapioca pudding. Having gone without breakfast, she had been hungry and had eaten a great deal more than she usually did in the middle of the day. She decided that she would spend the afternoon in bed and make another attempt to get involved in the unrealistic entanglements of Annabella and Derek and the others.

It was not until she heard the car sliding down the driveway that she realized she had chosen solitude. With Edith and the two hired girls gone, she was alone in Farview—except, perhaps, for Drew.

She became uneasy in the silence. Once more she could get no further than the first chapter of the novel. Within a very short time she was out of bed again, and, for some reason she could not quite explain to herself, was going toward the door to lock it.

That was when she heard the music. It came faintly from somewhere along the corridor, then broke off and was replaced by a mechanical-sounding voice like that of an announcer.

Somewhere in the house there was a radio, although she had not seen or heard one before. She opened the door and stepped out into the hall. She looked in the direction of the ell and saw that the door there was open. The voice was clearer now: "You have heard the one-minute newscast, on the hour every hour from station . . ."

Rosemary began to edge along the wall, keeping in its shadow. She expected the door to the ell to slam shut at any minute, but it did not. If Drew were in that place, which she had been warned not to enter—and it could only have been Drew, for there was no one else in the house—she could think of no reason why she should not go into it too.

She reached the open door and looked in. The odd arrangement of the rooms beyond it did not surprise her, because she and Drew had played in them on rainy days. They led off from each other with no connecting hall. To reach the farthest one, it was necessary to walk through the other three.

What did surprise her was the luxurious look of the place: comfortable chairs and a lovely old piecrust table and Persian rugs and a loveseat upholstered in gold brocade and a huge television set and lamps with carved bases.

She looked beyond the first room but could see little from where she was standing. She took a few tentative steps forward and then stopped short.

From a wing chair in front of the television set, hidden by its tall back until that moment, a man got up leisurely and crossed the room in her direction with long, easy strides. Poor as the light in the room was, Rosemary recognized him.

He was Martin Morse.

Chapter Ten

THERE WAS no mistaking that face, with its long jaw and prominent nose and deep-set eyes. There had been no pictures taken of Martin Morse for a number of years, but he had not changed to any great extent. His hair was streaked with gray and his neck, above an open-necked shirt, was somewhat crumbled. But he was, as he always had been, a handsome man. His eyes were a hard, smooth gray. They were staring intently at Rosemary now, and she felt the embarrassed flare of color in her cheeks.

"I am sorry!" She began to back away. "I did not mean—"

He silenced her with the wave of a long hand. "No, don't run off. Ever since last night, I've been hoping I'd see you again. I left the door open for that purpose."

His voice was compelling. When he gestured again, she moved further into the room. He moved around her and closed the door.

She was still feeling the effects of astonishment, and she said shakily, "Then it was you who picked me up when I fainted."

"Yes, child, it was me."

He drew forward a chair for her and she perched on the edge of it, her eyes fastened on his face. She was still scarcely able to believe that this was the eccentric billionaire about whom she had been reading since her childhood. Except for his imposing good looks, he looked like any ordinary man spending a quiet afternoon at leisure.

Her glance dropped down to his feet. He was wearing carpet slippers. She remembered something in a news story about one of his idiosyncracies being a hatred of shoes, and how he traveled, conducted high-level business meetings, and attended fashionable parties in his bedroom slippers.

He grasped the back of the wing chair, turned it around, and sat down facing her. His gaze was making her uncomfortable, and she dropped her eyes. Beside the chair was a pile of books; others, as well as magazines and newspapers, were scattered about on tables and the tops of cabinets.

"Tell me about yourself, who you are."

It was an authoritative voice, almost harsh. It softened when he said, "I asked one of those maids about you this morning; which one, I can't say. They look alike to me. All I got was an evasive answer, and Edith hasn't been up here yet today. Who are you?"

She explained. Although her throat was dry at first, she found she could speak more easily as she went on. She told Martin Morse why she was in Farview and, feeling that she owed him an explanation for having fainted, what she had seen from her window the night before.

He listened without speaking, without even a change of expression. When she had finished, he reached over and took her hand. He held it in a gentle clasp.

"You should not be here," he said in a voice that was firm at first, then softened as he went on speaking. "Not that I want you to disappear, now that I've seen you."

She sat mute and shaken by the words as his eyes moved slowly over her hair and her features.

"You are very like her, you know. The way she was when I first met her." Then he asked abruptly, "You know who I am?"

The question brought a quick smile to her lips. "How could I not? You were supposed to have vanished. The papers have been full of it for weeks. There have been all sorts of rumors and speculations and conjectures—in the papers, on television. I'd have had to be blind and deaf."

He breathed a deep sigh. "Of course. All that wretched publicity. I never wanted it, but I couldn't escape from it. Will you be too bored if I talk about me?"

Rosemary's feeling that it was all not quite real grew stronger. She could not believe that she was here in this forbidden part of the house with a man whose name had become a national byword and that he was actually asking her permission to confide in her. She could do nothing except dip her head in a nod.

"If you think it's the story of the typical poor little rich boy, forget it," Martin Morse said. "I worked with my father in the oil fields from the time I was fourteen. I was eighteen when he struck it lucky, twenty when he died and left me all the money he had been piling up. I was lucky, too—investments, buying up an airline. The right place, at the right time." He shrugged.

"The rest of it—what you may have read—was all phony. Well," he admitted, "to be honest, maybe it was a kick at first. The heady feeling of power. The lovely ladies with dollar signs in front of their eyes. But I didn't find anything that made life worth living until ten years ago— when I met Marianne."

He was speaking very softly, and his eyes had grown soft with a faint look of sadness.

"She was my wife—the only one I ever had, in spite of all those crazy rumors about secret marriages. She looked a lot like you—the same color hair, the same look of gentleness and, well, vulnerability. I shielded her as much as I could from the publicity. Many of my closest business associates never met her. They didn't even know about her death until long after it happened. We had a place in the Bahamas. She was buried there. It was the last thing I could do to protect her."

He fell silent, and Rosemary sat quietly while he remained absorbed in his old sorrow. When he looked up finally, there was a dim smile twisting his mouth.

"Now, why am I telling you all this?" he said. "It's the resemblance, probably. I haven't talked to anyone like this for years. Rosemary—I must call you that, you know—why didn't your aunt tell me about you? She promised to keep my being here a secret, but she must have known that I'd want to meet you."

"As to that—" she began, then broke off.

"You mean, what am I doing here? Is that what you were going to ask?" He waited for her to nod, then went on. "I knew Edith Gilbert years ago. She was one of the New York crowd then. One summer—it must have been eighteen or twenty years ago—she invited me up here. When things got too bad, when I couldn't stand the pressures any longer, I remembered this place. I got in touch with Edith and asked if I could come up and hibernate for a while. That's all it was. No great mystery about it, just what the newspaper boys dreamed up."

His eyes had returned to her face, and he said, "I'm no great believer in fate. You have to make what luck you get. But I'm ready to admit that something brought us together here in this place."

She opened her mouth before she realized that she had nothing to say. His smile came again, wider this time.

"That startled you, dear? Forgive me! I've always been an impatient man. My competitors have always described my methods as roughshod. We'll drop this, for the time being. But we'll see each other again. Be sure of that."

It seemed like the right time to end this strange and disturbing conversation. Rosemary got up from her chair and walked toward the door. She found him there before her. He put both his hands around hers and lifted them and kissed them. It was a strange, old-fashioned sort of gesture, and when she went out into the corridor and moved along the hall to her own room, she felt as though she were walking in a daze.

Chapter Eleven

SHE WAS not able to think straight for a long time. She remained in her room moving restlessly about, glancing out the window from time to time, although there was nothing to see except the trees swaying lightly in the wind. She tried to keep her mind and glance from that one particular tree with its hideous significance, but her eyes kept returning to it as though that black, twisted branch had the power of a magnet.

Now she wished that she had accepted her aunt's invitation and gone with her to the village. The meeting with Martin Morse had disturbed her. The things he had said to her hung persistently in her mind, no matter how much she wished she could rid herself of the memory.

Martin Morse had not cautioned her not to divulge his whereabouts to anyone. He seemed to have felt, without being told, that she would keep his secret. He must have felt confident of Edith's discretion, too, or he would not have come to Farview in the first place. She had guarded the secret well, had lied to Rosemary to keep her away from the ell. The two hired girls were aware that he was in hiding in those few rooms at the end of the corridor. They had served him his meals there, undoubtedly provided him with fresh linen and kept the rooms in order. Perhaps they were being well paid not to reveal his whereabouts.

Which left only Drew. Rosemary's thoughts went back to Drew once more. Whether or not he was aware that there was someone else living in Farview, she had no way of knowing. Her puzzlement was stronger than ever now. And in the silence, broken only by the faint sound of music coming from down the hall and the everlasting

70

thundering of the ocean, thoughts of leaving Farview began to take form in her mind.

They were tentative at first. There was the wondering: Why did I ever come here? There was the admission: It was a crazy sort of thing to do, a running away.

She had had to run away because she had not been able to face the wound to her pride and her disappointment over Tommy Ross. The thought of finding another job and another place to live had discouraged her, and she had believed that the old house overlooking the sea would be a sanctuary. But there had been no magic of healing, and Farview was not the same place it had been when she was a carefree child. What she had left behind began to seem infinitely better than what she had found here.

"And there's nothing to keep me here," she told herself half aloud. "If I had a single brain, I'd pack up and get out of this place, with its dead people who seem alive, where someone hanging from a tree vanishes before the next morning, and where open graves are booby traps for unwary people."

The resolve came gradually, grew stronger, and finally possessed her. She went as far as the closet and was pulling a suitcase out of it when she realized this was running away with a vengeance. Rosemary knew that she would not be able to simply take off without seeing Edith first, to explain, as well as she was able, why she did not want to remain in Farview. Ordinary civility demanded that much, and just exactly what she would say she did not yet know.

Edith had lied about the ell not being occupied, but Rosemary understood the reason. She had doubtlessly given her word to Martin Morse that no one would learn, by anything she said or did, where he was hiding.

That mystery was cleared up. But there were the other things, and Edith had not believed Rosemary when she had spoken of them. So perhaps she would decide that her niece was a strange sort of girl and that a sudden departure fitted into the pattern of her erratic nature.

The light outside the window was beginning to fade. It would soon be dusk and Edith, Rosemary was certain, must have come home by now because no one would

choose to drive up the deserted road that stretched from
Farview to the village in the darkness. Surely not in an ancient limousine that seemed as old as the woman who
drove it and looked, to Rosemary, like the gangster's car
in a late night movie.

She glanced at her watch and was startled to see that it
was well after six o'clock. Although she had not heard her
aunt return, she guessed that Edith was in her room by
this time, probably dressing for dinner.

But when she went along the hall and rapped on the
door of Edith's room, Rosemary received no response.
The house seemed very still. From where she stood, she
could not hear the music from the ell, and if there were
women in the kitchen, they were being very quiet in their
dinner preparations.

Her knocking sounded loud in the hushed house; the silence was so dense that all the people who had been in it a
few hours ago might have died.

Now, why did I think of that? Rosemary wondered uneasily. It was not the sort of thought to bring comfort in
this gloom-filled hall, with darkness gathering and night
only a little way off.

She twisted the doorknob and looked into Edith's bedroom. There was little to see, for its heavy draperies were
drawn across the windows and the frilly lamps on the
dressing table and beside the bed were not turned on. Nor
was Edith lying on the bed as Rosemary had half expected
her to be, resting after her trip to the village.

Rosemary went back to the staircase and had almost
reached its bottom step when she heard the voices of Lucinda and Bertha Swift coming from the kitchen. She
stopped and listened for a moment as her malaise, instead
of being washed away by relief, began to prickle coldly
along her flesh.

It was a minute or so before she realized why the sound
of two women talking together at the end of the day was
not the cozy, pleasant sound it should have been: the
voices were not the normal ones of Lucinda and Bertha.
They were missing the exaggerated Down East twang.

Rosemary went slowly down the remaining steps and

turned in the direction of the kitchen, expecting to find two strangers there when she crossed the threshold.

They sat at the table, the pair of sisters in their starchy housedresses and with their hair pinned to the tops of their heads in the usual severe arrangement. Lucinda was facing the door and quickly got to her feet when she saw Rosemary. Bertha twisted around to follow the other woman's gaze and pushed back her chair. She, too, arose and turned her back to the table as though to protect from sight what was on it.

Rosemary had seen nothing at all out of the ordinary there: a coffee pot which was half full, a few dirty dishes, a sugar bowl and creamer. Lucinda and Bertha had evidently been finishing their supper at the moment of her arrival. Rosemary could think of no reason in the world why they should appear so . . . She could not think of a word to describe the matching expressions on the two faces. It could not be guilt. There was no cause for them to be perturbed because she had found them at their evening meal, unless they had forgotten her, had not known that she was in the house and failed to prepare her supper.

Bertha's face became bland, and she spoke in a hasty rush of words that ended the awkward silence. "If you'll go into the breakfast room, Miss Rosemary, I'll bring you your supper there. I was meaning to bring you up a tray, but as you're down here now, perhaps you'll be more comfortable in there."

She was speaking too quickly, her smile was too determined, and the harsh twang was back in her voice. She lifted her hand and swung it toward the hall in a gesture that was peculiarly graceful. But Rosemary did not move. There was something disturbingly false about the little scene. The two women might have been playing roles in a muddled drama, with Rosemary as a spectator who had come in late and missed the beginning.

"What about my aunt?" she asked finally. "Won't she be eating with me?"

Bertha said, "But she isn't at home, Miss. She drove down to the village this afternoon, and she hasn't come back yet."

"That I know. You went with her, didn't you? Wasn't she supposed to drive you back?" Impatience was putting an edge on her voice. When neither of them answered her, it grew sharper and shriller.

"Well, wasn't she? She wouldn't have left you down there with no way for you to get home!"

"We came back in a taxi." Lucinda shrugged her narrow shoulders. "We usually do when we have an afternoon off. That way we don't have to depend on her to meet us. Don't worry about your aunt, Miss Rosemary. I'm sure there's no cause."

Rosemary had not been worried—merely puzzled about Edith's absence—until that moment. Her aunt must find life in Farview dull. It was only natural that she would escape from it occasionally, drive into one of the cities along the coast to shop or visit friends there.

There was that, on the one hand—a logical explanation for her absence—and on the other, the oddness of her hired girls' manners.

Rosemary could not understand why Lucinda had felt it necessary to reassure her, or why Bertha put in, "She does that quite often, you see. Goes off on these little jaunts and doesn't come home until late. Sometimes stays overnight."

Nothing that had been said so far had done anything to calm Rosemary's uneasiness. She was not at all cheered by the prospect of spending the night alone in this dismal house, with only the two women for company. And Martin Morse, of course, who had locked himself away from human company in the ell. And Drew?

She did not ask where Drew was, because she knew what the answer would be. She turned when Bertha gestured again and walked across the hall to the breakfast room. There was no more conversation while the two women served her. They had become once more the taciturn, impassive servants who did not speak unless they were spoken to, and then only in monosyllables.

When Rosemary had finished eating, she went into the living room and turned on the lights. She had two reasons for not wanting to go back to her room: an unwillingness to take a chance on seeing Martin Morse again, and a determination to stay up until Edith returned from wherever she had been.

The man had a compelling sort of charm. The things he had said had moved her more strongly than anything she could remember. That their meeting had affected him she did not doubt. But he was plainly of a romantic nature, and his self-exile must be unbearably boring at times. It might not be hard for him to feel an attraction for the first young female he had seen in weeks.

When she left him there in the ell, the matter was ended as far as Rosemary was concerned. Once she had seen Edith and explained her reasons for wanting to leave Farview, everything and everybody in it would be left behind.

And so she would sit here and wait for Edith to come home. That was her plan; but something beyond her control made it impossible.

The dizziness came first. She was sitting in an armchair, her head resting against its back, when the room seemed to dip and swing. She felt as though she were swimming in circles. Then the whirling became faster, spinning her in a thick black cloud which could, at any moment, swallow her up into oblivion.

She clutched at the arms of the chair so tightly that the bones of her hands began to ache. Then she pushed herself upward, staggered, and fell back into the chair.

With one remaining scrap of her brain still functioning, she remembered that people on the verge of fainting could fight off unconsciousness by dropping their heads forward between their knees. To move at all was an effort, but she managed to grasp her temples and force her head downward.

The spinning grew slower and stopped. She went on sitting there in that awkward position until her mind began to clear. Then she got up cautiously and, by leaning first on one piece of furniture, then another, made her way to the door.

The staircase leading to the second floor seemed to loom impossibly steep and high; she was sure that she would never be able to reach its top, for while her feet felt like lumps of lead her legs had no strength in them at all.

She fastened one shaking hand on the banister and pulled herself upward. There were only a few steps remaining before she reached the second floor when a pain, as hard and sharp as a steel blade, lanced into her stomach. It was the first in a series that made her double over, gasping.

For a few wretched moments she remained there, clinging to the banister, not knowing whether to go back downstairs and beg help from the women in the kitchen or whether to try to reach her room. The first twitching of suspicion sent her struggling upward and, still bent with the pains that were coming more rapidly, she reached the corridor, turned, and fell into her bedroom.

The nausea came then, weakening her still more. She was barely able to make her way to the bathroom before it overcame her. She was miserably sick for a long time, and her stomach became sore and aching.

When she went back to her room and fell across the bed, she had one lucid thought before surrendering to unconsciousness: she knew that she had been poisoned.

Chapter Twelve

SHE WAS supposed to have died. Someone had tried to kill her.

At intervals during that long night she floated up through the layers of a deep and unnatural sleep and the knowledge was there, ready to seize her muddled mind.

It was the only thing that came into it and it became part of a series of incessant nightmares that drenched her body with perspiration and dragged her back to consciousness from time to time.

She was not able to explore the premise or to give form

to her suspicions. She realized only that if the nausea had not come, she would be dead by now.

Once, during the night, she remained awake long enough to be aware of the heavy silence in Farview. Even the ocean was quiet, the sound of its waves a light murmur. She thought that she heard the chugging of a motor boat far out on the water; but when she thought back on it later, she was not sure whether or not it had been part of a dream.

Morning came in a burst of sunlight that stabbed her eyes and brought her suddenly awake.

The pain and the horror of the past night rushed into her memory. She touched her stomach gingerly and lifted herself off the pillow in a slow and careful movement. There was no more nausea and no more swimming sensation in her head. All she felt was weakness, as though all strength had been drained from her body. When she threw back the bedclothes and put her feet on the floor, her knees collapsed, and she sank down on the edge of the mattress.

She wanted nothing except to get back into bed and give in to her lethargy. But she fought off the temptation, knowing that there were things that she must do and that they had to be done as quickly as possible.

So she went on sitting there for a little while, then got up and tried once more to move around the room. It was better this time, easier to control her footsteps. She was walking almost steadily as she pulled a suitcase out of the closet, took down the dresses that were hanging above it, removed underwear and sweaters from the bureau drawers and packed them.

Whatever she did seemed not quite real; she seemed to be moving in a daze. Then she remembered that this was what she had planned to do the day before, in preparation for leaving. Her plans had been a sort of mental rehearsal for her leave-taking. She had intended to tell Edith. . . .

Rosemary's thoughts veered in another direction when Edith came into them. Surely her aunt had returned by this time. And now, she was determined, there would be no shilly-shallying, no searching for the tactful words, the trumped-up reasons to explain why she had to get away from this ghastly, danger-filled house.

She would say bluntly, "Your hired girls tried to kill me."

Edith might be shocked, incredulous, even angry at the accusation. Or, perhaps, believe that her niece was, in truth, suffering from some sort of mental aberration. It would not matter. Rosemary would say what she had to say and leave.

She left the luggage—her large suitcase and the smaller weekend case—beside the bed, then went down the hall and knocked on Edith's door. When there was no answer, she opened it and peeked in.

The room looked exactly as it had the last time she had seen it. The bedspread was smooth, the draperies were pulled across the windows, there were no articles of clothing in sight. Rosemary was certain that her aunt had not spent the night in her frilly, feminine boudoir, which had, now, a deserted and desolate look.

A thickening cloud of worry was gathering in her mind. She went downstairs quietly and slipped out the front door without meeting anyone or hearing sounds of occupancy from the kitchen. Wherever Bertha and Lucinda were this morning, they were not anywhere on the first floor.

Outside, on the grounds, the wind was gentle. There were birds high up in the branches of the trees—the first sign that spring had finally come—but Rosemary heard their raucous quarreling with only a small portion of her brain. Her concern about her aunt's absence was growing stronger. She was walking rapidly as she turned the corner of the house and went in the direction of the little structure that had once been used to shelter horses and carriages and was now a garage.

She went into it with a little twitching of dread, hoping that she would not find what she feared. But she did. Edith's big, old-fashioned limousine was gone.

Rosemary's car looked somewhat lost, standing as it did alone in the shadows. And where, she wondered, had Edith gone after she left the two women in the village?

What had kept her, and was still keeping her, from returning home?

A parade of possibilities formed in Rosemary's mind: an accident on the dark, narrow road that ran the length of the peninsula; a sudden illness had overtaken her; some minor trouble with the ancient car had left her marooned somewhere.

But if any of those things was the reason Edith was missing, surely word would have reached Farview by now. She had gone off shortly after lunch the day before—eighteen hours ago.

The thought that was plaguing Rosemary was the memory of her own wretched illness. But if Edith had been affected by something she had eaten at noon, she would not have been able to drive her two servants to the village a short time later.

Or had she? That was not necessarily what had happened simply because they had said so. The statement could have been false, just as everything else about them, Rosemary was beginning to realize, was false.

The garage, with its old smells hanging on the fetid air, was bringing back a feeling of queasiness. She struggled to fight down a threatened assault of nausea, forcing herself to open the door of her car and climb into it.

There was something she knew that she must do, and she was determined that nothing—left-over illness, apprehension, or dread—would keep her from doing it.

She intended to drive down the peninsula road and make sure that there was not a huge, old limousine drawn up on the side of it with a woman who had been unable to drive any farther, helpless in its front seat. Helpless, or dead.

The picture was so sharply outlined in Rosemary's mind she could almost see that big car gleaming in the sunlight and the body of a woman slumped over the steering wheel.

A feeling of urgency began to press upon her, and she took her car keys from her sweater. But when she turned the ignition, nothing happened. There was no sound of the motor coming to life. Turning the key again and again and pressing the gas pedal availed nothing at all. Her first feeling of puzzlement changed to anger.

There had been nothing wrong with the car when she arrived at Farview. It had not been driven since. She had put it away ...

But she had not. Because when she went downstairs to garage it, Drew had been there, and she had given him the keys because he said that he would take care of it.

She remembered that little scene with disturbing clarity and recalled what he had said to her. There had been that question about why she had come, and he had hinted that she had expectations of a legacy.

That had nibbled at her mind on another occasion. She had wondered about the fortune Henry Gilbert might have left and the succession of his heirs.

Edith would inherit, in the natural order of things; then, if she were to die, the estate might fall to Rosemary. But, if Rosemary were to die before her aunt, then it might be that Drew would come into the money and the house and whatever there was of value left in it.

If that were so, Edith would have had to make a will in Drew's favor, since he was not actually a relative but the son of her second husband. And perhaps, Rosemary thought with a squirm of fear, Edith was being held somewhere until she, Rosemary, was dead, and then she could be forced to sign a new will.

It was utterly absurd, she realized a moment later. What she had done, in her imagination, was form a coalition of murderers: Drew and the two hired girls plotting to kill her first, then Edith Chester. The women were strangely mannered, engaged in some sort of masquerade, and undoubtedly they had poisoned her food. But she could not see Drew in that light. He had sometimes made her miserable with his taunts and rudeness when they were children. Yet there had been no cruelty in his nature. She could remember how tenderly he had taken care of a bird fallen from its nest, how he had nursed a sick and filthy stray dog he found on the beach, the way he had ministered to her own scratches and bumps and bruises.

Her head was beginning to ache. She pressed her fingers

against her temples as though she could quiet the beating in them. This, too, was like a nightmare: disjointed, raddled, one mounting horror expelled by the one that followed it. She began to feel sickened again by the smell of old wood and dampness.

She tried once more to start the car, failed, and gave up with a little sigh of despair. She got out and walked back into the sunlight, drawing deeply into her lungs the clean, salty air.

At the edge of the lawn was the cliff that fell to the ocean. She started in that direction and then stopped, remembering the open hole she had fallen into and which had come so close to being her grave. Drew had saved her; if what she had been thinking about him a little while ago were true, why had he not left her there to die instead of saving her life? She moved forward slowly to see if the hole was still there. It was not. She crept a little further toward it and saw a fresh mound of dirt with swards of grass atop it. They were uneven and there were spaces between them, as though they had been thrown there hastily after the hole had been filled in.

The oblong looked like a fresh grave, and Rosemary stood staring at it in the paralysis of horror, wondering who was buried under that newly formed mound.

Chapter Thirteen

HER MIND was in chaos as she turned and raced toward the house. At first it was only a witless flight, a running away from what she had seen there on the lawn, but by the time she reached the steps, the clamoring in her brain was becoming fainter.

She knew what she must do, what she probably should

have done when she first suspected that her life was in
danger. In spite of the fact that Farview was a remote and
isolated place, it was still part of a world governed by law
and by law officers who could be appealed to for protection. She had only to pick up a telephone and call the police to ask for help from the danger that threatened her.

Where had she seen a telephone in Farview? She could
remember only one, and that was on a wall in the kitchen.
She rejected the thought of using that one; she did not
want to run the risk of meeting Bertha or Lucinda or of
being overheard when she put in her call.

Surely there would be another one upstairs—perhaps in
Edith's bedroom. Rosemary did not recall having seen one
there, but both times she had been in the room she was
upset and had not seen anything with any great clarity.

The house was still quiet when she went in. Everyone
else who had lived in it might be dead and she the lone
survivor in this place, which had been like a haven to a
small girl many years ago. The thought was not a reassur-
ing one, and she went quickly past the closed doors on the
first floor and hurried up the staircase.

She was silently rehearsing what she would say after the
operator connected her with whoever was the head of the
police department in this part of the world. Sheriff? State
Police? She tried to think back to when she had been in
Grist Mill Corners as a child. She could remember only a
stout man in a short-sleeved shirt and sun helmet directing
traffic on hot summer days, when the influx of tourists and
vacationers was at its peak.

When she entered Edith's bedroom and looked around,
she felt a heavy plunge of disappointment. There was no
telephone on the bedside table, where she had expected to
find one. Or on the dressing table, or on the lowboy, or
anywhere at all.

Across the room was an open door, which she had not
noticed before. When she went to it and looked through it,
she saw a little room that adjoined the larger one. In contrast to the neatness and order of Edith's, this unfamiliar
place was shockingly untidy and cluttered. And it was full
of strange things.

There was a chipped old bureau against one wall, some of whose drawers stood half opened and spilled clothing. At the opposite wall was a table, covered with stained oilcloth, with a stool drawn up to it; over it was a mirror bordered by electric light bulbs. A closet door stood open, and Rosemary could see old garments that looked like costumes of some sort hanging there.

She walked closer to examine them. She found out-dated evening gowns, a long white robe trimmed in tarnished silver braid, a velvet cloak with a ruffled collar. There were other things, all jammed in together—plainly the accumulation of many years.

Curious and puzzled, she went to the top drawer of the bureau, opened it, and released from it a jumble of play bills, dead flowers that fell apart when she touched them, newspaper clippings turned gray and almost illegible, champagne corks and swizzle sticks, and a wine glass with the name "Edith Gilbert" traced in silver letters on it.

As Rosemary emptied the drawer, taking out each article, looking at it, then placing it on the top of the bureau, she saw a leather-bound scrapbook at the bottom. She lifted it out, opened it, and found pasted on its pages other clippings and a few faded pictures.

The photographs were of her aunt at a much earlier age, her hair arranged in a way that looked ridiculously old-fashioned, her poses theatrical. Rosemary glanced at them briefly and then began to read the clippings.

They all pertained to Edith Gilbert, reviews in which her name had been underlined with a red pencil. Some of them were favorable; in others, she was mentioned only in the last paragraph as a member of the cast.

The book was only half filled, and the dates under the reviews were those of twenty and thirty years ago. Edith Gilbert, as she had been known then, had had a fairly short professional career.

And this, Rosemary realized, was what seemed to set her aunt apart from other women, made her seem more glamorous and exciting. She had not understood during her childhood summers—or perhaps she had known, and it had made no impression upon her—that Edith had been an actress.

She looked through the other clippings. None of them were underlined. Friends, Rosemary guessed, or fellow actors and actresses—those lighthearted and fun-loving guests who had filled Farview with their bright voices and laughter during the summers when the stage had been in the doldrums.

She took out the telegrams that had lain under the scrapbook and saw that the names on them were, in some cases, the same as those in the clippings. "Good luck, darling" "We'll be out front rooting for you" "Break a leg . . ." "Know you will be a great success."

When Rosemary had finished reading them, she replaced everything in the drawer. Her mind had been absorbed by the souvenirs of her aunt's career as an actress, and it was several minutes before she could bring it back to the present. She glanced down at her watch and became appalled at the time she had spent in this room, with its relics of another age and a different way of life.

This was not why she had come up to Edith's room, and for a long while, she had forgotten her purpose. She had been looking for a telephone and had not found one. The knowledge that she desperately needed help came back in all its force. And she could not think where, or how, she was to get it.

In this empty house . . . The thought broke before the sentence was half finished. Farview could not be completely empty. In the ell at the other end of the corridor, there was a man who was hiding from the world. In spite of the fact that he had exiled himself from it, he was one of the most influential men in America. She had only to appeal to him, and he would either find a way for her to summon the police now or arrange a way for her to leave Farview.

And so she crossed Edith's room, went down the hall, and knocked on the door that led to the ell.

Martin Morse answered the rapping as quickly as though he had been standing there waiting for a visitor. He was in shirtsleeves and Rosemary, glancing down at his feet for no reason, saw that he was wearing his well-worn carpet slippers. She had been feeling a little embarrassed and at a loss, now that she was there, about what to say.

His unconventional footwear, oddly enough, was the means of putting her more at ease.

"You've read about that, too, I imagine." He put his hand above her elbow and led her into the place he was using for a sitting room. "All sorts of rumors on that score, too. I'm supposed to have club feet, a fungus growth, no toes, and other things too numerous to mention."

His laugh was a pleasant sound, more like a deep chuckle. He said, "They never found out the truth. I told it to Marianne and she thought it was a great joke. I broke my foot when I was—well, eighteen or so. Dropped a piece of machinery on it. I started to wear slippers out of necessity, then found they felt so comfortable that I saw no reason to go back to shoes. Now I don't even own a pair, and these feel great."

He held out a chair for her and sat down opposite her, looking directly into her eyes. His face had grown sober and his voice was gentle as he asked, "What's troubling you, Rosemary? This isn't an ordinary social call, is it?"

"I need your help, Mr. Morse!"

He edged his chair closer to her, leaned forward, and picked up one of her hands. "You'd better tell me about it. What is it that's bothering you?"

"The fact, first of all, that I need to use a telephone. Privately. And I haven't been able to find one. Mr. Morse, please! Do you have one here?"

An uneasy look spread across his face. "No. It was one of the things I wanted to get away from. Look, don't keep calling me 'Mr. Morse.' I should be Martin to you. No nickname. Even the papers didn't dream one up for me. Well, let's have it—the reason you need to make a call."

She hesitated for a moment, uncertain about how much to tell him and undecided about how to begin. And then the words seemed to come of their own volition, and she told him everything. She started with her arrival at Farview and the feeling that she'd had about there being some other life below its surface. She described the changes she had found in the house, none of them for the better. "I remembered it as luxurious and comfortable, not run-down and shabby the way it is now."

She described finding Henry Gilbert in bed in his room, although the man had been dead for two weeks and she had seen his grave in the churchyard in the village.

Martin did not move during the recital. He sat leaning forward, his hands clasping hers, his eyes intent on her face. His features seemed to leap and tighten when she recounted having seen a body swinging from a tree on the grounds.

"Roland Harmon!" There was an edge of defiance in her tone. "I know, you don't have to tell me. He was kidnaped five years ago and has never been seen since. I couldn't have been mistaken, and I did not dream that."

Martin made no comment, and she went on. She told him of the open grave she had fallen into and the fact that it had been filled in during the night. And how something had been put into her food to poison her and that her aunt had been missing for the past twenty hours.

"Something must have happened to her! She wouldn't stay away this long unless she couldn't—couldn't come home. Those two women. . . ." Rosemary choked, and it was a few minutes before she could control her voice and go on. "I'm sure they're at the bottom of all this. They seem to be missing, too. Have you seen them yet today?"

"Come to think of it, I haven't." Martin's eyebrows drew together in a frown. "But there's nothing strange about that. I have a refrigerator back there," and he motioned with his head to the room that led from the one where they sat talking. "And a hot plate. I often get my own breakfast and make coffee whenever I feel the urge. You say they're gone?"

"I haven't seen either one of them this morning. Oh, Martin, if you know anything about what's going on in this place, will you please tell me?" Her fingers tightened around his hand. "So I'll know what I'm up against. I realize that everything I've said sounds unbelievable, but I hope you will—believe me, I mean."

He picked up her other hand and pressed it against the

one he held with his strong ones. "Good God, child, I had no idea anything like this was going on. But what makes you stay?"

She explained about her car. "And the road—oh, how could I walk all that distance carrying two pieces of luggage? I don't know anything about the tides, when they're at their highest and that sort of thing. It may be that they flood the road."

He sat looking at her without speaking. There was a wry grimace twisting his mouth, and she guessed that he was thinking that all his power and influence and fabulous wealth could do nothing now to give her the help she needed.

"I wanted to be cut off from everything," he said sardonically. "It seems I succeeded only too well. As for those two women, they were paid and paid well to wait on me whenever I needed it and to keep their mouths shut about my being here. I never dreamed, of course, that I'd meet someone like you here."

Disconcerted, she slid her eyes away from his. "I don't understand," she murmured, "why you picked this place. There have been those stories in the newspapers about your being on an island in the Caribbean or hiding in the Florida Keys and in Canada—oh, lots of different places!"

He laughed shortly. "I've seen them. They brighten up my days. As to why I came here, Edith and I are old friends. I met her when she was in show business, and she invited me up here one summer, about—let's see, fifteen years or so ago. You must have been no more than a toddler then." His smile was for her now, faint and tender. "And I didn't know, of course, that you were in the world."

"I was seven," Rosemary said with dignity. "Not exactly an infant." And because the conversation was becoming too dangerously personal, she changed the subject. "How did you get here?"

Edith, he said, had met him at the airport and driven him to Farview. He had not noticed much of his surroundings that night. He had been too concerned with keeping his whereabouts secret, and he had not seen the deterioration of the house which Rosemary had spoken about. And since he had been in it, he had left the ell for the first time only when he carried Rosemary to her bedroom.

"I may as well be honest with you. I had been feeling myself on the verge of a nervous breakdown. And I was afraid that the news of my mental condition would become public and affect certain business deals I was trying to pull off. I left everything in the hands of an assistant, and even he doesn't know where I am. Rosemary," he said gently, "I have to tell you all this because when we're out of here it isn't, you know, going to be the end of things for us."

She did not know what to say, and so she said nothing. She drew her hands out of his and stood up. He came to his feet quickly and looked at her with an expression of anxiety on his face.

"It won't matter, will it?" he asked. "I'm healthy enough. Not a candidate for one of those places politely called rest homes. I don't intend to let the pressures get me down again. I might very well sell out everything and enjoy life; but I couldn't do it alone."

She started toward the door, but he put his hands on her shoulders and turned her around to face him. "What do you intend to do?"

"What I started out to do, find a telephone. You must know, from all I've told you, that I must find a way to get out of here."

"You won't leave without telling me?" he asked anxiously. "I'll want your address, where to reach you."

She was about to tell him that she had no address and had no idea where she would be. But she thought it might sound like a further bid for sympathy, and she knew that a large part of what he was feeling for her was protective solicitude. Because she was young and in danger, and because she might resemble his dead wife, it was he who was vulnerable—the word he had used to describe the girl he had loved and lost early in life.

Rosemary promised that she would come to say goodbye after she had found a means of leaving or had put in a call to the police. She started down the hall and had almost reached the staircase when she heard someone coming up over it. She drew back into the shadows of a recessed door and peered out.

And she saw Chotsie Metcalf turn and disappear into the darkness at the other side of the corridor.

Chapter Fourteen

SHE DID not have to search her memory this time. With her very first glimpse of the girl, Rosemary found the name that went with the sharply planed face, its prominent cheekbones and wide mouth, and the cascade of white-blonde hair.

Chotsie Metcalf had been almost as well known as Martin Morse and much more cooperative with the press. Six or seven years ago, scarcely a week passed without her picture and a write-up of her escapades in the newspapers.

Her life style had been anachronistic in an era when young people were turning serious, marching, demonstrating, even risking their lives in the cause of justice. Their new set of values did not include the senseless spending of money which represented Chotsie Metcalf's way of life.

She had been a throwback to the days of what the newspapers termed "madcap heiresses." Although she did not go to the lengths of the high-spirited debutantes of the 1920s (as far as Rosemary knew, she had never dived into a public fountain or ridden a horse into a fashionable restaurant), she had managed to keep her name in the public eye.

The news then was almost as dull and depressing as it was now, and Chotsie Metcalf became the darling of reporters and photographers. She eloped with a prince from an obscure Middle-Eastern country, and the marriage lasted only a few weeks. She appeared at a night spot in a revealing garment which, she confided later, was a night-gown. She had a brief fling at singing in fashionable supper clubs and quit when she became bored. The parties in her Manhattan town house and her summer place in Newport were reputed to be the gayest and the wildest in history.

Chotsie had been photogenic, and there had been some talk of her going to Hollywood to make a film; but she was, at twenty-five, completely undisciplined. The industry was in deep trouble and no studio head could take a chance on her whims and lack of acting experience.

Her recklessness had cost her her life—or so it had seemed. She had taken flying lessons. The day after she received her license, she announced that she intended to pilot her private plane to Europe. And after she took off, neither she nor the plane had been seen again.

It had been taken for granted that she had perished in the Atlantic Ocean, and the search for any trace of her had monopolized the headlines for weeks after her disappearance. There had been reports that she had been seen in one place or another during the intervening years, all of which had proved false.

But what would Chotsie Metcalf be going in Farview? Rosemary watched the girl striding down the hall, the waist-long blonde hair that had been her trademark swinging easily.

She disappeared through the door of the ell at the other side of the corridor, and the sound of it shutting made a faint sound in the stillness.

"And Chotsie makes three." The silly phrase, a corruption of something from an old song, slipped into Rosemary's brain. There were three of them—people she had seen since her arrival who had disappeared amidst great flurries of publicity: Martin Morse, although there was a valid and logical reason for his having vanished; Roland Harmon, who had been kidnapped and never seen again; and now Chotsie Metcalf, who had taken off in her plane and presumably drowned somewhere in the Atlantic.

All three, as well as several others, had been in the

news account that Rosemary read in the little store in Grist Mill Corners.

She could not remember what she had done with the newspaper, and she was anxious now to reread that story about Martin Morse and the others to see if it contained any clue that the other two might still be alive.

Thinking back, she remembered that she had paid for the paper and then carried it with her when she went out to her car. So it must still be there, probably on the front seat. She was certain that she had not brought it into the house.

On tiptoe, she ran down the stairs and out the front door. She was breathless by the time she reached the garage. The sunlight was dazzling and she did not see, at once, the figure of a man standing in the doorway. She started when he spoke to her, then sighed, "Oh, Drew!"

For one confused moment, she did not know what to say to him. He was, in that space of time, two people: her friend and companion of years ago, and the man she had imagined plotting her death with two strange women who seemed to be engaged in some sort of masquerade.

He was staring at her anxiously. She could feel the coldness in her face, and because she had never been very good at hiding what she was feeling, especially in Drew's presence, she blurted, "Where have you been all this time? What have you been doing?"

Whatever he had expected her to say, it couldn't have been that. His mouth fell partly open and surprise made his eyes look blank. He took a step forward and put out a hand, but she backed away and lifted her own hands, holding them with their palms turned outward.

"Why, Rosemary!" he murmured. "You sound like a nagging wife. I didn't think you cared."

The light words did not cause any change in her expression. She could feel the trembling of her lips and the scald of tears with which she had to struggle to keep from spilling out of her eyes.

"What is it, girl?" His voice had turned grave. "Something more been happening while I've been away? Come on, tell me."

"No! I won't tell you anything because I asked you first." It sounded childishly petulant, even to her own ears, and she became silent for a little while. Then she said, "Never mind. It's none of my business, of course. I can guess where you were."

He appeared uneasy, and his glance slipped away from her. He seemed to be about to speak but then evidently thought better of it, because his jaw clenched and his hands dropped to his sides and became hard fists.

"It's nothing to me," Rosemary said with a shrug. "I'm not a kid. And certainly not shocked that you're having an affair with some girl in the village and spent the night with her."

Drew threw back his head and roared a noisy laugh. A moment later, he was gasping; when he could control his voice, he cried, "A girl in the village! Good God, you idiot, where did you ever get an idea like that?"

At first she wouldn't answer him. Then, when he threatened to shake the truth out of her, she said, "Bertha. Or maybe it was Lucinda. Anyway, they were both there. And Aunt Edith said it was so. Drew, believe me, I don't care one way or the other. I just want to clear up some of the strange things that have been happening."

He appeared not to have heard the last sentence. There was a peculiar look in his eyes, hard and glittering. Rosemary could sense his anger but knew that it was not directed at her.

"Edith said that, did she? And put those two odd characters up to lying, too? Well, you can tell her for me . . ."

"I will, when I see her again," Rosemary broke in. "Drew, she hasn't been around all day, and I'm tremendously worried about her. She's been missing since yesterday afternoon. Can you possibly have any idea what happened to her, where she is?"

"Missing!"

He repeated that one word and then growled, "How would I know? She's scarcely spoken to me since I got here. She made it plain that she didn't want me around. I had a winter vacation coming to me, and on impulse I drove up. She made me feel as welcome as an invasion of termites. And the more she hinted that she'd prefer my absence to my company, the more determined I was to stick around and find out why."

"And did you?"

The uneasy look was on his face again, and his eyes did not quite meet Rosemary's. He said curtly, "No!"

"But you must know where she might be. You didn't, by any chance, see her car anywhere along the road to the village? Or hear of an accident of any kind?" She persisted. "It's the only thing I can think of that would keep her out all night."

Once more he barked, "No!" and then purposefully changed the subject.

"What else is new around here? Nothing more happened to you?"

"Only that somebody put poison in my food last night, and I was miserably sick. And the big hole down on the lawn has been filled in. And that I've seen people, a couple of them, who are supposed to be dead around this place."

She knew that he would ask her who they were, and her mind clicked with a sudden decision. She was not going to tell him about Martin Morse, who was hiding from the world in the rooms he was occupying in the ell. She could not remember whether she had promised not to reveal his whereabouts or whether he had taken it for granted that she would keep his secret. When she thought about the man who had kissed her hand and treated her with old-fashioned courtesy and hinted that he was attracted to her, a flush warmed her cheeks.

"Still blushing?" Drew did not sound amused, and his eyes remained sober. "What is getting you flustered now, my darling?"

"The thought that you're not going to believe me," she lied. "It sounds too fantastic, but I hope you will—believe me, I mean."

She drew a long breath. "The man I saw hanging from the tree out there," and she gestured in the direction of the grounds. "He was Roland Harmon. You remember? He was kidnapped five years ago. His parents paid a huge ransom, but he was never returned and they gave him up for dead long ago."

Drew made a choking sound deep in his throat, and she lifted her head defiantly and said, "Just a little while ago, when I was upstairs, I saw Chotsie Metcalf going into the ell on the west side of the house. She was flying her own plane over the Atlantic."

"You don't have to remind me of Chotsie Metcalf. I was in college when she was doing her best to turn the world upside down. I had a roommate who had a crush on her, and her pictures were all over the walls on his side of the room. He went into mourning for days when her plane went down. But Rosemary," and his voice grew more gentle, "you could not have seen her. Somebody who looked like her, maybe."

"It's hopeless!" She threw her arms out in a gesture of futility. "I knew you wouldn't believe me. And I'm sorry I ran into you. All you're doing is upsetting me more."

"Sorry?" he asked softly. "Not relieved that I'm back?"

She refused to be coaxed into revealing that she was glad he was there. It was true that there was a special sort of feeling between her and Drew. But she was not going to let it wipe out the fact that he had not answered certain questions she had asked him and might be lying about other things.

He had not told her where he had been the night before. And there was that thing about his being unwelcome in Farview, which needed explaining. She spoke of that aloud.

"Why wouldn't Edith want you here, when she wrote to me so urgently and almost begged me to come?"

His shoulders rose and lifted in a shrug. "Maybe she likes you better than me."

"That's a foolish answer if I ever heard one!" she snapped. "Drew, why can't you be honest with me? I need —I need a friend right now."

He reached for her, but she pulled away. "A friend," she said stonily. "I don't want to be made love to or be given the 'There, there, little girl' treatment. Don't slough me off by telling me to split as soon as I can, because my car won't start and I couldn't just take off without know-

ing whether Edith is dead or alive. That grave!" Her voice
trailed off in mounting horror.

He shook his head impatiently. "No way! What you're
thinking couldn't have happened. You think someone
killed her?" he demanded with brutal bluntness. "Dug a
grave for her that she couldn't help seeing? You told her
about falling into that hole, so she knew it was there?"

Without waiting for her to answer, he went on speaking
harshly. "You can put that nutty idea right out of your
head. It's not that way at all. There's some other explanation, but I haven't got it yet.

"And by the way," he added. "you haven't told me
what you're doing wandering around out here. What were
you looking for?"

She told him about the newspaper story she had read in
the store at Grist Mill Corners. "I wanted to look at it
again, see if there was anything I didn't know about those
two people—the Harmon boy and Chotsie Metcalf. And
now, if you'll excuse me and let me by, I'll do what I came
in here to do."

He stepped aside and then went with her into the
garage. The sight of her car standing alone there puzzled
her. She turned to Drew and asked, "And where's your little sports job, by the way?"

The light from outside splashed shadows on the far wall
of the garage; when Drew stepped in that direction, his
figure grew dark and she could not see his face. It was like
being in that gloom-spattered place with a stranger.

When he spoke, his voice sounded odd, too—strained,
and slightly evasive. He said, "A little way down the road.
In the bushes, where it can't be seen."

Chapter Fifteen

ROSEMARY'S HANDS, which had been on the handle of the car door, fell away. She turned slowly and looked at Drew, waiting for an explanation. He plainly did not intend to give any because he said, with one of his abrupt changes of topic, "What seems to be the matter with your crate? Maybe if I take a shot at it . . ."

He broke off as she moved further away from him. "Hey, what is this?" he asked with a note of anger in his voice. "One minute we're on a pals and buddies basis and the next, you're backing away as though I've turned into Boris Karloff at his worst. Rosemary," he asked sharply, "are you afraid of me?"

"Not afraid." She chose her words carefully. "It's just that I've been having a rough time of it. And that should be a winner in the Understatement of the Year sweepstakes. Let's just say that I don't know what's going on or who I can trust or why you act the way you do and refuse to answer certain of my questions."

"Such as?"

"Such as why you would run your car into the bushes beside the road."

He seemed troubled for a few minutes. He ran his fingers through his hair in a gesture that she remembered him using when he was perturbed or was trying to remember something. He could not be searching his memory now, so the finger combing must mean that he was deeply agitated.

When he spoke again, there was something like an appeal in his voice. "I don't want to talk about it right this minute, because I've got to keep quiet about it for a while.

Until I'm sure. Honey, there's no question about your trusting me, is there?"

She refused to plead. He can keep his secrets for all of me, she thought with resentment seeming to touch her raw nerves. He could go on treating her like an idiot child, refusing to share whatever knowledge he had about Farview and its people. Except that it might have something to do with the danger that was threatening her, she did not care about anything that he preferred to keep to himself.

Moving away from him, she returned to the car, yanked open its door, and looked into the front seat. The newspaper was there, folded neatly so that only part of its headlines were in view. She slid out again with the paper in her hand. When Drew reached out for it, she gave it to him silently.

He unfolded it and glanced at the front page. "Another of those big jewel robberies," he said, his eyes running over the news account. "Been quite a few of them lately."

She could not guess whether or not he was deliberately trying to aggravate her. She sounded shrill when she answered him. "Not that, you dunderhead! That other story. The one that starts off about Martin Morse."

Her voice quavered a little when she said Martin's name. She had thought that Drew was engrossed with his reading, but he looked up and stabbed her with a keen glance.

"What's with the tremolo, love of mine? Why did you get all breathy and girlish when you said the Morse guy's name? Are you feeling wistful? Do your dreams include marrying a millionaire? Get in line, honey. There are thousands ahead of you, and you'd get lost in the crowd."

Little you know, she thought, smothering a smile. Aloud, she said waspishly, "Don't be any sillier than you can help!"

He went back to reading the newspaper. When he had finished with it, he handed it back to Rosemary. She looked through it swiftly, lingering only on the paragraphs pertaining to the others who had dropped from sight and never been seen again. There were six of them under a subheading that read: "DEAD, OR STILL ALIVE AFTER MYSTERIOUSLY VANISHING?"

The names listed were Chotsie Metcalf; Roland Harmon; Judge Jonathan Kalman, who had walked out of his courtroom one day and never been seen again; a housewife named Jennifer Myatt, who had disappeared while on a shopping trip; and the conductor of a symphony orchestra, who had not shown up for rehearsal one afternoon—or anywhere else after that. The sixth was Jared Dana, a young movie star who was supposed to have died in a car crash ten years before but who was rumored not to be actually dead, because the body taken from the wreckage had not been recognizable.

He, like all the others, had been reported seen in dozens of places for years. There would be a little flurry of publicity, which died down quickly when the person seen proved not to be the right one. Pictures usually accompanied the news stories, old photographs dug out of the files and used again and again until it seemed that every man, woman, and child in America would be familiar with the faces of the missing.

Drew had been watching Rosemary silently while she skimmed through the article. He did not speak until she had refolded the paper and tossed it into the car. Then he said, "Well, what now?"

"That's up to you. I won't leave until I know what's happened to Aunt Edith. What I want is to get in touch with the police and report her being gone. And I thought —well, I'm in danger here. Couldn't they give me some sort of protection?"

"What they'll give you," he said bluntly, "is a horse laugh. It isn't 'they,' by the way, but 'he.' Except during the summer, when there are auxiliary police to take care of the vacationing crowds, there's only Sim Briggs. He's the whole department, and I can just see him coming up here on the strength of what you've told me."

"It's all true!" There was a cutting edge of anger in her voice. "When it all first started, Edith told me I must have dreamed it. Tell me the truth, Drew: Do you think I'm a little nuts, have hallucinations?"

"No, but I can't guarantee that Briggs wouldn't. You've got no proof, nothing but a weird-sounding story to tell him."

She sighed and said, "The possibility has occurred to me—that I might be going crazy, I mean. And that someone is deliberately trying to drive me out of my mind."

Drew's hands went out and locked themselves around her waist. He pulled her close to him, and she let her head drop against his shoulder.

"That'll be enough of that kind of talk. Cut it out," he ordered gruffly. "What would be the sense of anyone doing a thing like that?"

When she began to speak, the words were muffled against his jacket. She lifted her head. "To get me out of the way. For the same reason that someone tried to kill me."

"And why," he asked patiently, "is it so important that you be removed?"

The ugly suspicions took possession of her mind and she pulled away from him, her lips tightening against her teeth and her eyes staring hotly into his. She did not intend to tell him what she was thinking, but he said, in the peremptory tone he had used when they were children and he had ordered her about, "Well, let's have it! You're holding something back, and you're not going to just leave it at that. Why are you so sure that someone is trying to put you out of the way? Don't give me another listing of the things that have happened to you. Just let me have a reason!"

Feeling like the small girl who had trailed after him and meekly obeyed his orders, she murmured, "Because of the money."

The expression on his face looked genuinely bewildered. "How's that again?"

"My grandfather's fortune. He could have left some of it to me, and if I—if I died, or had to be committed to a mental institution—"

Drew let her go no further. "Am I hearing what I think I'm hearing? Put it in simple terms. There are only you and Edith left of the family, right? So what you're saying is that she, in some way or other, wants you disposed of so she'll get the whole boodle."

Rosemary couldn't bring herself to look at him. Her voice was weak and shaky when she said, "I can't believe it of her. But except for me, you're the only relative she has."

There was a long, awkward silence; then he took her face in his hands and tilted it upward so that she could not avoid looking into his eyes.

"Do you actually believe that?" he asked softly. "I have to hear you say it first, and then I'll tell you something you should have guessed by now. All right, let's have it."

Her heart was thudding heavily as she studied him. The old feeling that everything he did was right, that everything he said was the truth, came back in a warm flood that calmed her agitation. He was not in any way remarkable. He could be cruelly blunt, but she had always been aware of his honesty and strength.

She spoke in such a low voice that he had to lean forward to hear what she was saying.

"No, Drew. I guess I never believed that you would—would harm me. I wouldn't be standing here like this if I did."

"Thanks for the vote of confidence." His lips unlocked and he smiled at her. "You know how I feel about you. Rosemary?"

She shook her head. "I don't want you to try to charm me or reassure me that way. I want you to tell me why the idea that I may be in someone's way is so far-fetched. Greed is a valid motive, isn't it? A strong one?"

"Sure enough. But it doesn't come into use here. There isn't any money. Your grandfather was up to his neck in debt when he died."

Chapter Sixteen

AT FIRST she thought that Drew must be in one of his teasing moods. But there was not the twinkle in his eyes or the sardonic twist on his mouth that she had seen when he was at his most exasperating. He looked grave and concerned.

She whispered, "Oh, surely not!"

"It's the truth, honey. He had a long, long illness. At the end of it, he had nurses around the clock. It seems he'd been living on his capital for years."

Rosemary, still incredulous, shook her head. "But the house! And he owned all the land along the peninsula. I think I remember that, don't I? There was a barrier across it at the point where it ends down near the village. I was pretty set up by that when I was a kid. I knew only rich people could be that exclusive. Edith had servants, still does. There were parties, all her friends were entertained here."

Drew put out his hand, clasped it around one of Rosemary's, and led her out of the garage. While they were inside, the sun had slipped behind a bank of heavy, dark clouds, and the grounds looked dismal and deserted. When they were on the path that led to the house, Drew stopped and pointed at the big, bleak structure that loomed beside them.

"Do you think the place would look like this if there was money enough to fix it up? I've seen the deterioration, the small economies, the penny-pinching."

"Not in everything," Rosemary went on arguing, in spite of the fact that she knew there was little basis for contradicting the things Drew had said. She thought of

something and seized on it. "Edith still has servants.
Those two women who work here. She said they'd been
with her for a long time. Forever is what she said."

"Then she lied."

"But why would she?" Rosemary protested. "What
would be the point in telling a falsehood like that?"

They were walking down the driveway by that time.
The rustic settee under a twisted old tree came into view,
and Drew led her to it and pulled her down beside him.

"Five or six years ago, one summer when I came back
here, there were those people—darned if I can remember
their names—a man and a woman and their daughter.
They were the ones who stayed on for a long time. You
should remember that, too."

She said she did and that what Edith had said about
Bertha and Lucinda had puzzled her, too.

"There was one year when there was no help at all, and
that was pretty grim. Edith isn't exactly the domestic type,
and it turned out that I was getting my own meals and
making my bed and doing the work around the grounds.
Needless to say," he added wryly, "my stay was a short
one."

Rosemary asked, "When did you first see the two hired
girls?"

"When I got here this time. Three weeks ago, just before your grandfather died."

He stopped speaking and looked at her with a question
in his eyes. He might be waiting, Rosemary thought, for
her to take up that subject; but she was not going to repeat
that story of having seen Henry Gilbert in his room long
after he had died and was buried.

"The day I came," she said, "the day I met you in the
driveway, you said something about an inheritance. Well,
actually, what you asked was whether I had come in the
expectation of being an heiress. If I expected all this," and
she waved in the direction of the house, "to fall into my
hot little hands."

"Good Lord, sweetie, don't you recognize a joke when
you hear one? It was a rib." His astonishment seemed
real. "I thought you'd take it the way it was meant. I

thought, too, that you knew how things were here, your aunt's circumstances."

"I did not. I had no idea. Because I never came back after that last summer, thirteen years ago. Why did you, Drew?" She turned and looked at him. "What brings you here? If you had, as you said, a vacation coming to you, why not a ski lodge or a Caribbean cruise or a couple of weeks in Florida?"

"That's the way you see me—a playboy in the fashionable places?" He grew sober immediately, and his voice flattened. "Edith was married to my father. They were never what you'd call blissfully happy because she couldn't get the acting bug out of her system. But she was kind to me, as kind as she could be considering how self-centered she was. She brought a little taste of glamor into my life. I felt I owed her something, even though she had divorced my father shortly before he died. This place isn't all that far from New York, and I've always liked being here. Until this time," he added.

"And why did things change between you and Edith?"

Rosemary asked the question without expecting a satisfactory answer. Nor did she receive one.

"I haven't the slightest idea." There were the lines of a frown between his eyes. "That's what keeps me here now. I'm a week overdue at the office. But I know something's wrong here, that Edith is in some sort of trouble, and I don't mean only financially. And I can't just take off," he said simply, "and leave you behind."

She realized that her hand was in his, and she drew it away quickly. There was a pleasant little shimmering in her nerves, and when she spoke, it was not in answer to what he had said but about a different subject.

"I'd forgotten, if I ever knew, that Edith was an actress. When I went looking for her in her room, I came across another little place that must be her dressing room. There were all sorts of things in it: an old scrapbook, pictures, souvenirs. Drew, was she successful at all? Did she make it on the stage?"

"She had a couple of good parts, I think. I saw her once when I was about ten. My father took me to a matinee. I was a little too young to understand much of what I saw and heard, but I got the idea that it was a pretty bad play. She went on the road for a time, but you know what's happened to the theatre. She always had this place for a cushion, came back after both her divorces. And brought all her friends. You remember how lively it used to be?"

"That's exactly the way I remembered it, what I expected to come back to." Rosemary smiled fleetingly. "Well, I learned one thing. The world changes. You can't go back to the carefree days of your childhood."

She sat quietly for a while, her dark thoughts matching the gloom of the day now that the sun had been smothered by the lowering clouds. There was a chill from the breeze that swept up from the ocean, and Rosemary felt herself shivering. Then Drew's arm went around her.

"You shouldn't be sitting out here in only a sweater," he said in his masterful manner. "It looks like it may rain at any minute. Can't have you catching a cold." He drew her closer to him.

She laughed shortly, because catching a cold would be the least important of the things that had happened, might still happen, to her. She felt safe and warm in the circle of Drew's arm.

They began to talk easily, like old friends catching up with each other's lives during the time they had not seen one another. She asked about his job, and he told her that he was an architect with a firm in mid-Manhattan. When he, in turn, wanted to know what she did for a living, she confessed that she was, at the moment, unemployed. "And homeless, too."

That led to Daria and Tommy Ross, and she was surprised to find that she could talk about them easily, without the familiar feeling of hurt pride.

"You're toting around a broken heart?" Drew asked. "You're in mourning for your lost romance?"

Her laugh was silvery and unforced. "Hardly! It never would have gone much further between us, anyway. All right, it's your inning. Who did you leave languishing behind? Anyone?"

"No, on my honor. Or down at the village, either," he said a little grimly, "no matter what you may have heard."

The world came back then. It had been a pleasant little interlude of easy conversation and a pushing aside of the doubts and the fears and the suspicion. But it could not, of course, last any longer.

"Why would they tell me, Edith and those two women," Rosemary asked, half to herself, "that you had come back because you were in love with a local girl?"

"I've told you I don't know."

"Or why Edith doesn't want you here?"

"That, too."

For a little while she was silent. Then she squirmed out of his arms and stood up.

"No matter what, Drew, we're going to have to do something. We can't just go on sitting here when Edith is —well, who knows what? We're going to have to try to find her, anyway."

"Okay, boss, where do we start? Let me have a suggestion. Have you been all through the house?" he asked. "The old place is full of little cubbyholes. What about the ells? Did you look in them?"

She said, a shade too hastily, "She wouldn't be there. Why would she? The day I came, she warned me to keep out of the one that's on the side near my bedroom. She said it wasn't safe, that a good storm could cause it to collapse."

It was not actually a lie. She had only quoted what Edith had said. She did not know why she felt impelled to keep from Drew the fact that Martin Morse was hiding in those rooms, and she found that she had not been completely successful in her attempt to turn his thoughts away from that part of the house.

He barked, "That's hogwash! She must have had some reason for not wanting you to go in there. Suppose we—"

She interrupted him, putting her hand on his sleeve with a tighter grip than she realized. "We're wasting time. Edith isn't in the house. Her car is gone."

He looked at her with an odd, uncertain expression. "And the other ell?"

"Not now. Drew, can't you go and get your car? And that, by the way, is something you haven't explained. Why did you feel you had to hide it?"

He mumbled something about it being his only link with civilization and being afraid that what had happened to hers would happen to his.

"But you didn't know about mine then!" she persisted.

"I know. I just wanted to make sure it was out of the reach of—someone."

It was all she could get him to say on the subject. When she demanded, "Were you sitting there spying?" he answered, "Something like that."

She wanted to ask him if he had seen Chotsie Metcalf driving up the road while he had been sitting in his hidden car at the side of the road. But the easiness between them had vanished. She had not told him the truth about who was staying in the second floor ell, and he was being tight-mouthed and evasive again.

"I'll go get the car," he said, "and drive back and pick you up. It's a fair walk, and you don't seem too robust today. Wait here, and I'll be back in a little while. Then we'll see if we can find Briggs."

He went away then, and she went back to the rustic seat and sat down. The wind had sharpened, and it tossed her hair and whiplashed her cheeks with its chill. A cold shivering spread through her body, and she got up and walked up and down the driveway in an effort to keep warm. She could hear the waves breaking in a rising roar against the rocks at the foot of the cliff, an ominous sound almost like a human voice shouting threats.

She kept looking at her wristwatch, wondering why it was taking Drew so long to walk partway down the road and drive back. Time was dragging, made slow by her own uneasiness and fears. If he did not return . . . .

But he was coming, she realized at last. With a rush of relief so strong that she tottered a little, she started up the driveway when she heard the drone of a car motor.

Then the vehicle came into view. It was not, she saw in horror as it came speeding down the driveway, Drew's small sports car.

It was a Volkswagen bus, and it was headed directly at her. She jumped backward onto the grass and it swerved to follow her. She stumbled and fell limply like a rag doll, her throat locked and all her senses stunned in what she realized were her last moments of life.

Chapter Seventeen

SHE COULD not remember, later, what had happened after that instant when Death was inches away. It was to remain only one of a series of sounds that penetrated the overwhelming terror. The grind of brakes. The squealing of wheels. The motor, loud only a second before, growing fainter and then becoming lost in the distance.

Drew found her there. Those were the final sounds, his rushing footsteps coming across the lawn, his voice shouting things that would not have been fit for her ears if she had been able to hear them clearly.

The voice sounded far away, dim, and then became lost as she was released from the numbness and a searing pain shot along her leg. She gasped and then was still, beaten into unconsciousness by the pain and the horror and the throbbing of leftover terror.

When the blackness of oblivion released its hold, she opened her eyes and saw the face of the man who was cradling her in his arms. It was chalk white, and its features were cast in such stony grimness that they might have been carved out of marble.

He asked, in a voice she had never heard him use before, "Are you hurt?"

He tried to lift her to her feet, but a hot, swift lance seemed to be stabbing her knee and she fell against him. He tightened his grasp and carried her to the wooden bench, lowering her into it. Kneeling beside her, he put his fingers on the spot to which she pointed and touched it gently while she told him what had happened.

"Sprained ligament, most likely," was all he said.

It seemed to hurt him to talk. His teeth were clenched and there were white lines at the corners of his mouth. When he said, "No place else, though?" his voice was rough and angry.

"A few bruises, maybe. The grass was soft." She was surprised at how calm she sounded. "I had a lucky, narrow escape."

"That you did, girl. So it would seem. But he couldn't have actually meant to kill you. You understand that, don't you?" There was no softening in the grim tone. "Don't ask me to explain it. What it seems like is some sort of campaign of terror."

"Drew, why?" The cold shivering had returned. She could feel it all through her body, even in her fingertips and her feet. "He stopped—I think—only inches away from me. It's all a jumble in my mind now, but I do remember that. Then he backed away, took off."

They had both said "he." So she knew that Drew must have seen the little bus, too, and its driver. He began to ask her about that, and she said, yes, she had seen the man at the wheel. Only for an instant, not long enough for his face to have become imprinted on her brain. He had been wearing a soft hat with a wide brim that shadowed his features.

"Men don't wear that sort of hat anymore. Or any at all, most of the time. I think it's called a fedora, and you see them in the old movies on TV."

She was babbling, sounding the way she felt—lightheaded and giddy. "You must have seen them, too. And him. Did you get a good look at him, Drew?"

"He flew by me on the road. I saw the bus—a Volkswagen, wasn't it? I knew a man was driving it, but when I tried to flag him down, he turned his head away and picked up speed."

She could hear the stuttering of rage in his voice when he said, "They did something to my car, too. Siphoned out the gas that was in it. That's why it took me so long to get back. I had to walk both ways."

Then he asked abruptly, "Do you think you can make it to the house? Leaning on me? If not, I'll carry you."

She put out her hand to him. "Drew, what are we going to do?"

"I haven't figured that out yet. But something, you can be sure of that! I am not going to stand still," he said, spacing his words far apart for emphasis, "for your being scared out of your wits, made a patsy for some weird reason, almost run down. His brakes might not have held. You could have been killed. Well," he suggested, not seeming to realize how ridiculous the advice was, "put it out of your mind."

That brought a dim smile to her lips. It was quickly gone, though, and she muttered, "Whatever you say. Drew," she asked, pointing to her knee, "what am I going to do about this?"

"I'll get you up to your room and then bring you up some ice. You can make a pack, and that'll ease the pain and keep down the swelling. And after that, I'm going to call Briggs and turn the whole thing over to him. There's a phone in the little room your grandfather used as a study. It's on a table behind the door. You wouldn't see it unless you knew where to look.

"If I have the time, before the police get here, I want to take a good look around that room, see if I can find out what he left and to whom. I could be wrong; there might have been something of value that he left. If you were the legatee then Edith might be the next in line. I thought there was a good relationship between them, although he was pretty rigid and old-fashioned in his thinking and never approved of her two divorces. There could, you know, have been a serious quarrel that made him change his will."

"But that's awful!"

Rosemary was leaning on his arm as she limped up the driveway beside him. She stopped short and looked at his stern profile.

"What you're saying is that it's Edith who wants me dead."

"Or put out of the way by other means. That's been in my mind—why I've been hesitating to talk to the police. You've been seeing things no one else has seen. A mound of dirt that you think might be someone's grave, but could be explained away as a garden plot that somebody has been digging. That would all sound pretty nutty, and all it would need is the next of kin to sign the committal papers and a couple of doctors to examine you."

He moved his head in her direction and saw the expression on her face. He muttered, "What a fool I am to scare you with this sort of talk. It's only a wild guess, and I should have kept my mouth shut. And besides," he said, lying valiantly Rosemary knew, "Edith herself is missing. But once we find her, everything will be cleared up."

But the frightful things he had said were not wiped away from Rosemary's mind that easily.

"You know it isn't true," she whispered. "That I'm not—I'm not mentally deranged. You'd be on my side, wouldn't you? If it came to that? You'd tell them that I wasn't imagining all those things, not hallucinating? They'd listen to you."

They had reached the steps, and he slipped his arms around her and carried her over them. He put her down carefully on the floor of the porch and, still holding her, looked into her face.

"No, my darling, don't bank on that. I'm in love with you. It must stick out all over me. I never was a guy who could change my face easily. One look at me is all it takes to know what I'm thinking. What's the cliché—heart on the sleeve? I couldn't be near you and not let the whole world see that I'd do anything at all for you, even lie."

"Drew!" He wasn't teasing now. It wasn't one of his put-ons. "I never suspected . . ."

"Don't give me that nineteenth century coyness! And don't, for Pete's sake, tell me you think of me as a brother. Or a friend. Once we're out of this mess, you're going to find out how unbrotherly I can be. As for being friends—

sure, that'll be part of it. But there'll be much, much more. Like this."

His mouth came down and covered hers, then he straightened up again. As brief as the kiss had been, it had shaken her. She said weakly, to explain her trembling, "You're not playing fair, Drew. I'm in no condition for emotion-charged scenes."

"No, you're not, are you?" he agreed cheerfully. "But there'll be plenty of time."

And with his arm around her waist, he helped her through the front door, across the hall, and over the staircase. She felt the stillness in the house and said, lowering her voice, "I wonder where they can all be. I know there's someone in that other ell—or has been."

"We'll find that out, too," Drew promised. "The first order of business is to get this injury of yours taken care of."

They were making the turn at the second floor hall. When Rosemary glanced down into the shadows, she saw with a tinge of dismay that the door to the ell there was open. She limped forward hurriedly, hoping that Drew would not notice. But there was a news broadcast on Martin Morse's radio or television set, and the newscaster's voice was clear in the hush of the corridor.

". . . last night in Boston . . . police estimate the robbery involved several hundred thousand dollars in jewelry . . . a witness, whose name has not yet been made public . . ."

Rosemary did not hear the rest, because she had turned to look at Drew. The expression on his face chilled her.

The newscast was cut off abruptly after she had heard only a few words about an unidentified woman, the victim of a traffic accident on Route 91. She was torn between fear over the possibility that the woman might be her aunt and the necessity of getting Drew away before he learned who had been listening to the broadcast.

It was too late now. Her hands fell to her sides helplessly as she saw the tall figure coming through the door in their direction. She heard Martin Morse call, in a voice with unmistakable notes in it, "My dearest girl, where have you been? I've been hoping to see you all day."

His arms were outstretched and he could not have seen the other man at first. When he did, he stepped backward, a bitter look on his face.

Drew was already gone by then, striding in the direction of the staircase, his back looking stiff and straight and outraged.

Chapter Eighteen

She couldn't run after him. She had been thrown off balance when he abruptly released her, and the pain in her knee was sharp, swift agony. She leaned against the wall, gasping. She wanted to call, to beg him for a chance to explain, but he was moving rapidly, and by the time she regained her breath, he had made the turn at the staircase and was out of sight.

What was there to explain, at any rate? she asked herself hopelessly. He had seen Martin Morse come out of the ell, heard the term of endearment, and the lover's tone of voice.

She knew what Drew must be thinking. Even giving her the benefit of all other doubts, he must believe that she had deceived him. As she had, of course. She had been untruthful by omission—if you wanted to nit-pick, she thought. Not outright lies, but the concealment of the truth.

Martin called her name from somewhere in the ell. She hobbled toward it, still clinging to the wall. He was standing a little way into the living room, out of the light. He could see her plainly enough, she knew that; but he made no sign that he had noticed her uneven gait.

"Who was that? Why was he with you, his arm around you like that? You!" he cried, his voice shrill with accusation. "I thought I could trust you, at least. Now he's seen me. Now he knows!"

She waited quietly until his anger had cooled a little. What she was feeling, as she looked calmly back at him, was pity. He was spoiled and arrogant and unreasonable. His wealth had done that to him. For years and years he'd had only to make a gesture, say a few words, and everything he wanted was brought to him. He had only to smile at a woman, Rosemary guessed, and she would fall into his arms. Now he was probably feeling an emotion he had never had to feel before: jealousy. And it was making him act like a small child in a tantrum.

So she was patient. When he demanded, "Who is he? Who's that guy who was hugging you out there?" she answered him evenly. "Drew Chester, Edith's stepson. And he wasn't hugging me, he was helping me to my room because I hurt my knee and was having trouble walking without support."

He paid no attention to her explanation. He was not, at the moment, interested in anything which did not concern him personally. He stared at her hungrily, wanting to be reassured, wanting her to tell him that no other man in her life was important to her. He felt himself, she was sure, above competition. He was Martin Morse and what he wanted, he got.

"He's in love with you!" he said, still in that fluctuating voice which was womanish and high-pitched one moment, husky with rage the next. "He is, isn't he?"

She could not think of any reason why she should lie to him. Whatever was between her and Drew was none of Martin Morse's business. She said coolly, "I believe he thinks he is. At the moment. We were kids together for a few summers here. Maybe it's nostalgia, or something like that. What he feels for me, I mean."

"And you?"

"I don't know. I haven't had time to examine my feelings, and that's the truth. Mr. Morse—Martin, I mean," she amended when his scowl drew more tightly across his forehead, "will you tell me what you've seen and heard

since you've been here? Anything strange that you've noticed going on?"

He wasn't listening this time, either. He muttered,
"Now he'll run out and spill the whole thing. This place
will be lousy with reporters and photographers by tomorrow. I don't know why you let him come upstairs with
you. You could have managed by yourself, if you'd really
tried."

"Drew won't. I'm sure of that." And then, in an effort
to shock him out of his self-absorption, she said, "You
aren't the only person who's hiding here. I've seen Chotsie
Metcalf. You remember her?"

It took him a little while to answer. He had to come out
of his engrossment with plans, perhaps for another flight
and the necessity of finding a new place to shut himself off
from the world. He had to turn over in his mind what
Rosemary had said and identify the name she had spoken.

"You mean that crazy lady who pulled all those wild
stunts to get her name in the papers? Chotsie? I met her
once. Then I made sure to stay out of her way. She would
have used me for publicity purposes. What did you say
about her? Not that she's staying here?"

He looked at her with his eyes narrowed, as though he
suspected that this was some sort of trick. So he must have
gone through all his adult life unable to accept what was on
the surface, looking for devious motives. He could not
have had any friends, Rosemary thought with pity, because he would expect everyone he met to try to use him
in one way or another.

"Chotsie Metcalf is dead," he said curtly. "These stories
crop up every now and then. Someone is always claiming
that they've seen her."

She decided not to argue with him. Instead, she tried to
reassure him about Drew's having seen him.

"There's no way he can tell anybody anything. Both his
car and mine are out of commission. You know how much
attention anyone would get if he telephoned. Newspapers
must get dozens of crank calls. Besides, he'll be using the
phone for another purpose."

I hope, she added silently. I hope Drew isn't going to let

his peeve at me stop him from calling the police chief—
what was his name, Briggs?—and getting him up here.

Surely he wouldn't—or would he? Her thoughts veered
away uneasily from the shocked and angry expression on
his face when he caught sight of Martin Morse and the
things he had said to her both before and after her close
brush with Death. Brutally honest himself, he might not be
able to understand and condone lack of truthfulness in
anyone else.

Martin was speaking. "Let's forget all this, darling.
Come and sit down with me. I've got something to show
you, a picture of Marianne. I want you to see the resemblance between you two."

She told him, as gently as she could, that she did not
want to linger there any longer. What she was unable to
say was that she was hoping Drew, once the heat of his
fury had cooled, would come back and that she did not
want him to find her in this secret place.

"I've got to get some of this grime off," she explained to
Martin. "And do something about my knee."

He let her tell him, this time, about the little bus that
had almost run her down. At first he looked cynical, his
expression disbelieving; but he listened until the end, and
when Rosemary described what had happened to her
knee, he seemed to become convinced that she was telling
the truth.

But his worry was not so much for her injury as over the
fact that she might be planning to call in a doctor. "It isn't
the way Edith promised," he said fretfully. "She assured
me there would be no one here except herself and the two
women. God knows, I'm paying enough for this deal."

Rosemary left him on that note, her sympathy a little
tarnished by faint disgust. As she walked to her room, she
found that she could do so more easily. Her leg was still
painful when she put her weight on it; she wouldn't be
able to do any hiking, but she felt optimistic about its
being healed enough to let her go in search of Drew when
she had finished bathing and changing her clothing.

He must still be somewhere in the house—probably
sulking in his room, she thought. He could not have gone

away from Farview, since his car was useless. And it was beginning to rain. She heard the hissing and pelting of the drops against the windowpane, and when she went to look out, she saw the wet veil of the downpour. The glass rattled as though it were trying to free itself from the old wood and putty. A cold draft blew in through the crack where the window did not fit into its sill.

She could picture the road to the village. Within a very short time, there would be puddles big enough to drown in and the threat, on either side, of the waves, which sounded wild and high. Drew would not be foolhardy enough to try to walk the entire length of the road in a storm like this— not for any reason at all.

He would come, she kept telling herself as she sat in a chair with her leg propped up on the bed. However angry or resentful or outraged he might have been feeling when he left her, he would not desert her in that fashion.

When she heard, a long time later, the sound of footsteps on the stairs, she lowered her leg, got up from the chair, and hobbled to the door. She pulled it open and stood clinging to the jamb, disappointment and fear and surprise making, in swift succession, an upheaval of her emotions. It was not Drew who stood there in the gloom of the hall.

Bertha Swift's face was impassive. She came into the room with a tray suspended on her hands, walking easily and yet with something studied about her movements, as though she had rehearsed them.

Never had Rosemary heard the twang more pronounced than when Bertha said, "Seems you've had nothing to eat today, Miss. I've brought you something because I'm sure Mrs. Chester would be much upset did she know you've gone hungry."

She removed the dishes and tea pot and placed them carefully on the surface of the dresser. Then she turned and, with the tray swinging at her side, started out the door.

Rosemary called her back. "Bertha, where is my aunt? And where have you and your sister been all day?"

"Why, in the places we should have been. In the kitchen, or doing up the rooms, or in the laundry in the basement." She was managing to sound genuinely puzzled. "As for Mrs. Chester, we do not try to keep track of her whereabouts. That's none of our business," she added primly.

"But her car is gone and has been since yesterday! And if you know anything about that, you must tell me!" Rosemary cried. "I am very much worried."

Bertha made no answer. She edged further away, and when she had reached the hall, she said, "When you're finished with the dishes, you can leave them on the floor out here. I'll pick them up when I've served the gentleman."

So it was all out in the open now. She knew that Rosemary was aware of Martin Morse's presence in the ell. But there was no way of learning how because she strode away hastily, her long skirt flapping around her legs.

Rosemary told herself that she would eat nothing of what Bertha had brought up to her. She was not going to be that foolish again, after having been poisoned on one occasion and possibly fed some sort of barbiturates on another. But she was growing weak with hunger, and the smell of the tea was filling her with a craving that was almost like physical pain.

She could not keep away from the dishes on the dresser. She picked up the tea pot and poured out a cupful of strong, black liquid. She put a spoonful of sugar and a few drops of milk into it and lifted it to her lips. She tasted nothing odd or bitter about it but she did not drink it all. There were two rolls on a small plate beside a steaming bowl of soup. She ate one of them, not daring to take a chance on the soup, which could, with its tiny bits of onions and chopped tomatoes and an herb she did not recognize, contain some sort of ingredient that might affect her in a way she feared.

Nothing could be done to a roll, she was sure; and so she ate the other one. And sipped a little more of the tea. And that was the last thing she remembered for a long time.

She felt the drowsiness coming on, but there was no way to fight it. Her eyes became heavy and their lids were gritty. Blinking accomplished nothing. As her arms slid off the arms of the chair, she tried to lift them—without success, for her hands were like chunks of lead and moving them was too great an effort.

Giving in finally, she let her head fall against the back of the chair. She was instantly asleep.

Chapter Nineteen

"THAT'S ALL it was," she kept insisting. "I was tired. There was no poison in the food this time. After all I went through today, sleep caught up with me."

She hadn't heard him come into the room. She hadn't heard anything until she awakened to find him shaking her, and then there was his voice, rough and husky. He had tried to get her to her feet, and that was when she had tried to protest.

"It was nothing except a deep sleep. What I ate—well, you can see for yourself, if you're going to be stubborn about it."

She looked toward the dresser. The dishes were gone. When she asked him about that, he growled that no, he hadn't removed them. Why would he have? he demanded. "They made sure to destroy the evidence."

And then he said that she was a little fool to have taken a chance like that. She could have waited. He had gone into the kitchen openly and with no to-do and taken a bottle of milk from the refrigerator and a couple of apples from the fruit bin and half a loaf of bread from the bread box. In plain sight of Bertha and Lucinda, who had come back from wherever they had been. He had explained nothing to either of them and had simply left the kitchen munching on an apple, intending to bring the other and the bread and the milk up to Rosemary.

"You knew I wouldn't let you starve to death," he said harshly. "But you couldn't wait."

"You were gone a long time."

Then it was there between them, the way they had parted—his fury and disappointment over her deceit, and her embarrassment and inability to make him understand her reason for it.

Since she had no defense, she tried offense. "If you had done what you promised, I wouldn't have had to act like what you called me—a fool. You were going to bring me ice cubes, remember? And get in touch with the police. It's been hours."

"During which time you were busy with that guy in there." He jerked his head in the direction of the ell. "Right? He was as surprised to see me as I was to see him." Then his curiosity took over. "He is Martin Morse, isn't he? The billionaire who's been missing for the past few weeks? This is where he's been holing up?"

She told him what she had learned about Martin Morse and tried to explain why she had kept his secret. "I just—I just couldn't give him away. He was on the verge of a nervous breakdown. That's why he's here. If I'd told anyone, the truth might have leaked out and this place would be swarming with newspapermen."

"That's what you think of me? That I'd make a dash to the nearest telephone?" His mind veered to another subject. "Speaking of which, the one in your grandfather's study isn't working. And probably not the one in the kitchen, either. They've managed to isolate us completely. And with what's going on outside, there's no chance of getting to the village."

She glanced at the window. The glass was streaming with wetness and clattering under each onslaught of wind.

"We're trapped, good and proper," Rosemary murmured.

"Oh, are we?" Drew's chin thrust itself forward. "Not yet, my girl. They'll find it isn't going to be all that easy."

"They?"

"Let's not start wondering about that now. You're right, I *was* gone for a long while. I lost track of time. And I wasn't sure, at first, that I was coming back," he said candidly. "You had somebody else to take care of you. Not that any guy who has to run away and hide because he couldn't solve his own problems could do much about helping you with yours. That dawned on me when I was in your grandfather's den—study, library, whatever you want to call it."

He began to empty the contents of his pockets on the bed. There were slips of paper, a journal which looked like a small notebook, letters and bills.

She leaned forward to see them better, but Drew said with a discouraging shake of his head, "Nothing that means anything much. I only brought them up so you could see for yourself. The bills are unpaid. The letters are mostly from stockbrokers, asking him to send money to cover his investments, and from collection agencies. He had turned everything he could into cash—insurance policies, some of the land on the village side of the road, government bonds. And it wasn't enough. The house is heavily mortgaged, and he would have lost that, too, if he had lived long enough."

He pushed the clutter they made aside and sat down on the edge of the bed. "And if you're wondering why I bothered to bring this junk upstairs, it was because I wanted you to see for yourself that there was no fortune and, therefore, no need for anyone to want you out of the way because of the money."

He was quiet and thoughtful for the space of several moments. Then he said, "There was only one thing. He kept a sort of diary. He couldn't have had much to write, sick as he was, but he'd describe a snowstorm he saw from his window or the way the trees looked without their leaves. And he'd put down thoughts, his very simple philosophy. Like members of the same family owing each other loyalty and abstract things like that."

Drew got up and began to pace around the room, the fingers of one hand working in his hair.

"There wasn't any mention of anyone by name. It

wasn't a diary, you see, but a way of putting down what he was thinking. But there was one rather odd thing. He wrote it a few days before he died. Here, I'll show you."

He stopped walking and reached for the little journal. He opened it at the back and riffled through a few pages. Then he said, "There! You see it?"

Rosemary looked at where he had pointed. The few words did not signify anything important to her and because excitement had begun to rise inside her, the subsequent disappointment was stronger.

All that Henry Gilbert had written, on one of the last days of his life, was, "Last night I heard the motorboat again."

She glanced at Drew and shrugged. "So what? He heard a motorboat out on the water. Every second person seems to have a boat these days. The percentage is probably higher in places like this, along the coast. Why wouldn't he have heard one? What's so great about that?"

"I'll tell you, my dense and dumb little friend: that was written during the first week of March. Nobody takes a boat out at that time of the year. Especially not at night. Read it again."

She did not have to bother. She could remember well enough those seven words, even though she had closed the notebook and handed it back to Drew.

He said, more softly this time, "And notice the word 'again.' What I get is a feeling that he was puzzled."

"A Coast Guard cutter?" Rosemary put in. "They're out all year round, aren't they? Day and night, if they're needed?"

He shook his head stubbornly. "He would have recognized the sound of that. He'd lived here all his life. And if he had thought it was that, he wouldn't have bothered to write about it. No, dear, it means something, and I wish I knew what."

Rosemary felt a little stirring of memory. The word "motorboat" had edged into her mind and it was digging up what had lain under it. She spoke suddenly.

"The other night, when I was so heavily asleep, I heard

it too. I did, Drew. It was only a faint chugging, but I was sure then—and I am now—that that's what it was."

She clutched at one of his hands and he put his free one over her fingers, pressing them so hard that she winced. "But what does it mean, Drew?"

"It means that there's something going on here that we're not supposed to know about. The only thing that occurs to me is something so crazy that it's unbelievable. Too fantastic to talk about."

But he talked about it anyway. He seemed to be speaking to himself as he looked somewhere over Rosemary's head, his eyes dark and seeming to be turned inward, his voice low and controlled.

"There's this character in the ell. In hiding. And there are the other two you claim you saw, who've also been missing. Maybe what Edith's running here is a sort of hide-out for people who are supposed to have disappeared but didn't, actually, and have reasons of their own for not wanting to be found."

"You're right," Rosemary said frankly, "it *is* fantastic. Besides being full of holes. The thing I can't get around is that Edith wanted me here but didn't want you. If she's hiding Chotsie Metcalf, as well as—as Mr. Morse, why would she believe that I wouldn't get onto it? And it doesn't explain about Roland Harmon, who's dead now and could be buried in that hole near the cliff."

It was the first time she had said that aloud. And it brought the horror back into the room. She went on clinging to Drew's hand, and she could feel the hard beating of a pulse at the base of her throat.

"Or that thing about my grandfather," she whispered.

After a short silence Drew said, "You know something? We're acting like a couple of goops. What we should be doing is going down the hall and talking to Edith herself instead of trying to dope this all out ourselves. Put it to her straight. Make her tell us the truth."

"Edith!" Rosemary's faint cry was an indrawn breath.

"I think she's back. I heard a car come up the driveway a little while ago. Not too clearly because of the storm, but it sounded like that big old ark of hers."

He had been speaking in a matter-of-fact fashion, and Rosemary, incredulous at first, felt the kindling of anger. It thickened her voice when she said, "Why didn't you tell me that straight off? You knew I was worried about her. You come in here with a lot of unimportant chatter about motorboats and people hiding out, and all the time you knew that Edith was in the house."

It could have been an excellent start for a splendid quarrel, but Drew remained calm and, uncharacteristically, began to justify his not having told her of her aunt's return.

"I'm not completely sure. I didn't hear her come in, although she could have used one of the side doors. And I wanted you to see this stuff before you saw her again." He pointed to the pile of papers and letters on the bed. "I wanted you to know that there was no fortune, nothing of value that your grandfather left, so that wouldn't be in your mind—the thought that Edith's been trying to put you out of the way so she could satisfy her greed. How could you face her, believing that?"

"Thanks very much," Rosemary said on a note of bitterness, "for making my decisions for me."

She struggled out of the chair, pulling away from him as he tried to help her to her feet. When he said, "The leg's some better?" she did not answer him.

But his hand was tight around the flesh above her elbow as they went to the door. He opened it and led her out into the hall, threw a brief glance at the ell which was closed off now, and matched his footsteps to her slow ones.

There was not much light in the corridor on this almost-dark late afternoon. The door to Edith's room was shadowed in the gloom. Rosemary was about to knock on it, but Drew caught her hand in time and shook his head at her.

She heard it then, too, the murmuring of voices coming from somewhere on that side of the second floor. She and Drew exchanged glances and he nodded. She curled her fingers lightly around the doorknob, turned, and pushed it cautiously. There was a faint squeak and they stood there waiting, for a second or so, to see if the sound had been heard by whoever was in one of the other rooms behind closed doors.

A boudoir lamp burned on Edith's dressing table. It threw a pool of rosy light beneath it, but not bright enough for them to see very much except that there was no one in the room and that the bed was neatly made and showed no signs of having been slept in.

Drew released his hold. He went to the little table beside the bed and picked up something that had been lying there. He held it up silently for Rosemary to see. It was a pocket-sized transistor radio, which she had not noticed when she had been in the room before. And now she did not understand why Drew's face had taken on a lively expression and why there was this air of suppressed excitement about him.

The door to Edith's dressing room was closed. She pointed at it without speaking, and they moved quietly toward it, opened it, and looked in. It looked exactly as it had when she had first discovered it. The bulbs around the big mirror were unlit and there was a careless and untidy look about everything.

But this time there was a difference; a second door was cut into the opposite wall and was open now, and the voices were coming from beyond it.

Moving cautiously to keep out of sight of the people who were there in the place that must have been part of the ell, Drew pulled Rosemary along behind him.

When they reached the door, Drew flattened himself against the wall, moving only his head to see what was on the other side of it. Then he motioned Rosemary to come forward and slid away to let her move into the place where he had been standing.

She drew in her breath in a gasp that sounded as loud as a shout in the clamoring of her mind. Drew quickly put his hand over her mouth and she stared over it with eyes that seemed to have become filmed over with shock. She blinked them rapidly, and what was in that room in the ell came into focus again.

It was a large bedroom, larger than any she had yet seen in Farview. And yet it looked crowded. There were two men sitting on the edge of a large bed. Edith and two other women were lounging in easy chairs at various places in the room. Bertha and Lucinda Swift were sitting on the floor, their arms around their knees, in strangely youthful positions.

Each of them held in his or her hands a glass, and the sound of ice tinkling in them was almost lost in the clatter of their voices. The smoke of their cigarettes made a thick, gray swirl above their heads. Rosemary saw Bertha lift a tiny cigar to her lips, draw on it, and then remove it with a graceful gesture.

It was all part of the unreality, the feeling that she was locked in some sort of dream from which she expected to awaken at any moment.

She could see the faces of all of them when the two men stood up and went to a lowboy, where there were bottles and a pail of ice cubes, and began to mix themselves fresh drinks. The faces of the three women who lived in Farview: Edith Chester and Bertha and Lucinda Swift. And the others: Chotsie Metcalf, and Jennifer Myatt, a young housewife who had walked out of a department store a few years ago and not been seen again, except in the fancies of people who had reported her as being in one place or another.

The two men at the homemade bar were separated in age by at least thirty years. The one whom Rosemary recognized as Jonathan Kalman, the missing judge, seemed to be in his fifties. Jared Dana, the reckless, speed-loving movie star for whom thousands of fans still mourned, appeared to be in his late twenties. The lock of hair that fell artfully over his forehead and the slightly sullen expression on his face were the same as they had been when he was supposed to have died in a car crash.

Only the conductor of the symphony orchestra was not there, Rosemary thought wildly. Of all the people mentioned in the story that she had read twice, once in the store in the village and again in the garage, he was missing.

And Roland Harmon, who was dead. She had seen his body hanging from a tree. So he could not be here. Mr.

Harmon regrets . . . Due to a previous engagement . . .
Hope your party will be a success . . .

Rosemary could feel the rising hysteria bubbling in her
throat. With Drew's hand still against her mouth, her
laughter was choked off, threatening to strangle her.

She pushed away the hand and shoved him away with
her elbows. She turned and fled across the dressing room,
through Edith's room, and out into the hall. She was not
conscious of the pain in her knee or aware of the darkness
in the corridor. The only thing that possessed her was that
she had to get away, far away, from that place where four
people who were supposed to be dead sat drinking and
smoking and talking and laughing.

Chapter Twenty

DREW CAUGHT up with her before she reached the door of
her bedroom. He seized her roughly and shook her.

"Little nitwit! You could have blown the whole thing!"

He pulled her into the room and shut the door behind
them. She was still gasping for breath and her lungs were
aching as she panted, "But they're dead! All of them, except Edith and the two servants. They were in that article
I showed you—remember? Jared Dana, the judge, that
woman who was shopping . . . ."

Drew wouldn't let her go on. She expected him to try to
comfort her, but his voice was hard when he said, "Yes,
they are. So now we know."

He wouldn't explain that. She was surprised and a little
affronted when he took the transistor radio out of his
pocket and turned it on. He stood with his hand on the
tiny wheel, changing from one station to another, rejecting
a program of syrupy old musical comedy tunes for the

blaring of rock and roll music and then for a sports-of-the-week roundup.

He found what he was looking for finally, a news broadcast. When Rosemary tried to speak, to ask what he thought he was trying to do, he raised a hand and silenced her.

She couldn't understand the intent look on his face as he listened to a weather report: "Storm due to abate later this evening. Tomorrow will bring some weak sunlight, temperatures in the fifties."

That was followed by the reports of a ship foundering off the New Jersey coast and the rescue of its crew and something to which she scarcely listened about the jewel robbery in Boston, which she remembered hearing about on Martin Morse's radio or television set. There were more details, and her impatience mounted until her nerves seemed in danger of snapping.

"A witness, whom the police refused to identify, gave an account of the robbery, but his naming of the criminals was termed 'ridiculous' by the authorities. The owner of the store has not yet completed a list of the stolen articles."

At the end of that news story there was another, about a threatened strike of transit workers in New York, which Drew heard out with his chin set grimly. "About time," he muttered. "We haven't had one for a few months."

His thoughts returned to her abruptly. "If they knew we knew, they would kill us," he said baldly. "Because they are that desperate. There's no sense in our trying to fool ourselves. We're expendable. So the thing to do is get away from here right now. Like the man says, let's do it yesterday."

"Oh, Drew!" She was beginning to feel even more confused, bewildered, puzzled. "We've been all over this. There's no telephone working, it would be impossible for me to slough down that road."

He did not let her go on. His voice cut over hers. "You're forgetting one important thing: Edith is back."

She repeated in a blank tone, "Edith?"

"Which means that her car is, too." He sounded impatient, and he was already moving toward the door. "The chances that I can get it going are slim, to put it mildly. That old ark might be locked up tight, but still she might have left the keys in it. If she was in a hurry to get inside, that is, and either forgot or decided to leave them there."

Rosemary limped over to the closet and was snatching at her raincoat when Drew said, "Not you, my love. I'm not going to let you slow me down. Besides, it might not work, and then you'd have made the trip for nothing and that, with your bum leg, wouldn't be so good. What you do is stand there at the window and listen. If you hear me drive out of the garage, then you get downstairs as quick as you can. Lock the door after me and don't do any more poking around. Understand?"

She understood only one thing: that she was going to remain here in this spot alone, with her nerves strung like tight wires, while he was busy trying to find a way for them to get away.

"I don't think I can stand it." Her voice quavered, but all he said was "Force yourself!" sounding a little stern. And then he walked away from her, turned at the door, and warned her not to move until she heard Edith's car in the driveway.

He spoke more softly when he reached the hall. "It isn't easy when you've got a cripple on your hands." But he was faintly smiling, and she knew that this was the old Drew, the Drew who couldn't resist a thrust, who had always been bossy and high-handed, who had laid down his own rules, which she was not to disobey.

He had ordered her to lock the door behind him, so she did that. He had said, "Stand there at the window and listen," and that was what she did for a long time.

She kept looking at her wristwatch, which she discovered after a while was a mistake. She had tried to time him: a few minutes to get out to the garage, a few more to get the car motor alive, another few to get back to the house. The schedule, she realized, was way off. Thirty minutes had already passed, and there were no sounds of anything from outside the house except the rain, which had diminished to a sluggish patter, and the steady growling of the ocean. When an hour had gone by, her nervousness turned to panic. Drew, she was sure, would have given up by this time. He would not have sat in that old car for sixty minutes, hopelessly trying to start it. He would have come back long ago—if he had been able.

She tried to turn away the things that could have happened to him when they came marching into her mind. If she accepted the fact that he was not returning to the house because he could not, she would become completely lost in the madness of fear.

Face it, she told herself at the end of another half hour; you are waiting for nothing. There'll be no clatter of that old engine, no big, ancient limousine on the driveway. Drew is not coming back.

She tried to think of what the world would be like without Drew. Only a short time ago, she had seen him for the first time in thirteen years. But during that short time, he had come to mean something important to her. She did not believe in falling in love quickly, and he was nothing at all like the type of man she had believed would appear one day, with whom she would spend the rest of her life. He was painfully honest. Even when he tried to make love to her, he was gruff; he had no charm, and he was overbearing and dictatorial.

But the thought that she would never see him again shattered her. And now, she knew, she must do something to bring him back to her. The time was long overdue. For almost two hours, she had been waiting at the window for something that she was forced to admit was not going to happen.

She needed help, and there was only one person in this house who could give it to her. Martin Morse must have a telephone in his room. For all he had insisted that he wanted to be cut off from the world, there had to be someone who was in his confidence and to whom he spoke now and then. An emperor of finance as he was, as important as his money was to him, he would have some form of communication with his empire.

Rosemary went to the door and unlocked it. She glanced down the corridor in the direction of the ell where she had seen Edith and all the people who were supposed to be missing. She thought she heard voices coming from that part of the house, but she could not be sure because the pounding of her own heart was loud, and she imagined that she heard that, too, louder than any of the other sounds.

Martin Morse came to the door when she knocked on it. The room behind him was brilliant with light, and she wondered if this was another of his hangups, a dislike of darkened places.

He seemed glad to see her, his hands going out in a swift motion toward her. But when he looked into her face, white, she knew, and tight with the strain of her long wait at the window, he stepped back and gestured her into the room.

"What's bothering you, my dearest, loveliest girl?"

She wished he would not speak in such extravagant terms. She was not here for sweet talk and romantic games. He might well be bored with his books and his television set and radio; he would no doubt welcome the diversion of telling his life story again—the tragic death of his wife, whom Rosemary was supposed to resemble, and his reasons for fleeing from the pressures and problems of a very rich man.

But she did not have time for that now, and she asked bluntly, "Martin, will you help me?"

He said, without thinking, "Of course I will, little love. Anything at all." Then his voice drifted off and his face became wary. "Help you? How?"

She told him in a spate of words. She knew that she could not hold anything back, that he must hear it all if she expected him to understand the urgency of the situation. She had spoken for only a short time when he interrupted her.

"Drew? Is that what you said? This stepson of Edith's? What you're asking is that I try to help you find him. So that's how it is?"

His eyes had become stony. "Don't give me any hogwash about you two being old friends. You're lovers, isn't that true?"

"No, it isn't." Her voice stuttered with impatience. "Martin, will you listen to me? We discovered who was in the other ell, and whatever the thing in this house is, it's something secret and evil. And so he's in danger. He went out two hours ago to try to start Edith's car, and he hasn't been back since."

Martin shrugged and turned away. "So he probably changed his mind and took off without you."

"He couldn't! He wouldn't!" she choked. "Whatever has happened to him, it can't be something of his own making. Martin, please come with me. Please help me search for Drew!"

He was moving backward and stumbled over a chair and caught at it to hold his balance.

There was a frightened note in his voice as he said, "I could have had a bad fall, hurt myself. And that, you know, would be disastrous. Away out here, no doctors or hospitals for miles around. Rosemary, my dear, I don't want you to think I'm criticizing you. But I can't be upset like this over somebody I've only seen once in my life. Edith's stepson is nothing to me. I can't take a chance on running into those people you say are staying in the other ell. The thing I hope," he added, lifting a thumb to his mouth and gnawing at its cuticle, "is that this friend of yours hasn't let the cat out of the bag already!"

She was not going to get any help from him; she realized that now. What she could do for Drew, she must do alone.

Chapter Twenty-One

THE PARTY had moved to another part of the house. Rosemary, in her raincoat and with a plastic scarf tied over her head, stopped at the head of the staircase when she heard the sounds of loud voices and the rattling of dishes from somewhere downstairs.

While she had been talking to Martin, they had presumably decided to eat supper and had gone quietly down to the kitchen and the dining room. Once away from where Martin could hear them, they no longer were concerned enough to keep their laughter muted and their voices low-pitched.

Rosemary's blood began to chill. The fact that they did not seem worried about her or Drew, knowing that they were here in Farview, seemed ominous. Perhaps they were aware of how helpless she was. And as for Drew . . . .

She felt her scalp tightening. In that cold, near-dark place, with a strong draft of air coming in through a window somewhere on the first floor, she could not bear to think of what might have happened to Drew. There wasn't the slightest chance that he had simply been allowed to drive away unhampered. While everything that had happened had happened to her, there was the thing about his car. There could be no reason for its being tampered with except that they had wanted to keep him a prisoner here, too.

The tempo of the party had increased, she realized as she stood with her hand on the banister. Some of the voices sounded slurred. One of the men began to sing a risqué limerick, which was drowned in bursts of shrill laughter and fits of giggling.

If not over the edge of drunkenness, they were teetering on the rim of it. Rosemary heard the crash of a piece of china, then a warning in the voice she recognized as Edith's crying out, "Keep it down to a roar, will you? He doesn't know you people are here. We've got to be careful about that!"

And then someone came out into the downstairs hall, crossing from the kitchen to the dining room. It was a man, and he was humming—the man who had been singing a few minutes before. His footsteps were not quite steady, but Rosemary knew that if looked up he would see her there, her beige raincoat visible in the gloom.

He hesitated at the bottom step, seemingly undecided as to whether or not to try to climb the flight of stairs. Rosemary saw that much and no more. She turned and ran down the corridor blindly, too intent on getting out of sight to choose her direction.

When she stopped, her heart pumping, she found that she was in front of the door to Edith's bedroom. She turned the knob, made a small opening, and slid through it. The boudoir lamp was still on, and except for a martini glass on the dressing table and an empty bottle in the wastepaper basket, everything looked as it had earlier that day.

The door to the adjoining dressing room was open, and Rosemary went to the threshold and stood glancing around with a frown. In this small place there were changes. Two large hatboxes, one atop the other, were stacked against the wall. On the oilcloth-covered table under the mirror, jars and bottles were crowded together. A khaki jacket and a matching pair of slacks were thrown over a chair.

Rosemary picked up the garments and held them against her body. They would have been too big to fit her, but not large enough for a man. And, with a whirling of realization in her brain, she recognized them. It was in this sort of costume that Chotsie Metcalf had made the ill-fated journey in her plane.

She dropped the garments on the chair and went to the other side of the room. She removed the cover of the top-

most hat box and began to pull out the articles in it. There
was a white wig, cut short in the style she had seen worn
by the man she thought was her grandfather when she had
gone into his bedroom. Under it was an old-fashioned
nightshirt and a pair of false white eyebrows.

Digging down further, she found another type of wig,
the kind known as a "fall"; this one was a pale blonde, almost silvery in the weak light. She shook it out and it rippled gently, the way Chotsie Metcalf's hair rippled when
she walked.

Rosemary threw the things back into the box and, not
bothering to look into the one beneath it, went back to the
table under the mirror and examined the jars there. She
unscrewed their caps and found they contained putty and
grease paint and makeup of all descriptions.

Then, afraid and upset by what she had found, she went
through Edith's room and back out into the corridor.

Now, more strongly than ever, the necessity of finding
Drew pressed upon her. If she were discovered here, her
face and nervous movements revealing what she had
learned, there would be no more close brushes with death,
no more narrow escapes. It would be the end for her. Desperate and ruthless as they must be, they would not let her
go on living. She was confused by the things she had seen,
and there was no time now for puzzling and trying to
make order of her thoughts. She knew only that she had
stumbled into something so evil that her life was in
danger.

As she went down the staircase, on tiptoe and forcing
herself to move slowly, she could hear Edith's voice soaring over those of the others. There were snatches of
phrases: ". . . If he gets onto it, the whole thing will blow
up . . . what I've planned, been working toward . . . he's
my biggest chance . . ."

Somebody hooted, blurring her words. Somebody else
shouted, "If they were giving out prizes for greed, you'd
get the blue ribbon, Edith, my love!"

It was the beginning of an argument, and it sounded as
though they were all in it now, the stupid, meaningless
quarreling of people who have had too much to drink.

Their sentences were only half-finished. One of the men tried to beat down the voices of the others with a string of obscenities. A woman—Rosemary thought it sounded like Lucinda—began to snivel in self-pity.

They were in the dining room, which opened off the further end of the hall. So, if she were careful enough to keep her footsteps from being heard, Rosemary hoped she could make it to the front door. There was only one place where Drew might be. He had left, hours ago now, for the garage. She could not believe that it would have taken him all this time to get the old car started. But he might have worked on it for a long time, and then gone down the road where his own sports model had been hidden and poured gasoline into it from Edith's car.

It was the only explanation she could think of for his long absence. She would not consider for a moment the possibility that what Martin Morse had said was true; Drew would not simply have taken off and left her behind.

When she had almost reached the entrance door, she felt her toe strike something, and when she looked down, she saw the article at her feet. She stooped down, picked it up, and stood, shocked and disbelieving at first, staring at the little transistor radio that Drew had been carrying in his pocket.

He would not have been that careless, she knew that. And she knew that wherever he was now, he had not gone there of his own volition.

Chapter Twenty-Two

HER BRAIN was spinning with hideous, terrifying pictures. The body of Roland Harmon suspended from the branch of a tree; the hole in the lawn that had been empty

one day and filled in, like a new grave, the next time she
had seen it.

A campaign of terror, Drew had called it. But she knew
that it was much, much more than that. She had felt it
from the first, that sense that there was some sort of secret
life going on under the surface of Farview. She did not
know the true story of that life, only that she must take
flight from it. The rainstorm did not matter. The fact that
her leg still pained her and that the only link with the outside world was a long, dark, dangerous road was unimportant.

Thoughts of what Drew had intended to do when he left
her came back into her mind. If he had never reached the
garage, it might be that the key to the ignition was still in
the old limousine. If she found that was true—and she
prayed that it was—she might be able to get Edith's car
going. Then she would drive to the village, force Sheriff
Briggs to listen to her, and insist that he turn the house upside down, if necessary, to find Drew.

With the hardening of her purpose, she felt suddenly
strong, determined. She refused to consider the possibility
that she would not be able to start the car and carry out
her plans. When she pulled open the door and ran across
the porch, she was scarcely limping at all.

She saw that the rain had diminished to a light drizzle.
The trees and grass and bushes shimmered in it, and the
driveway was slick. But the steady downpour which would
have drenched her before she was half-way to the garage
was gone, and this was, to her, a hopeful sign.

The door of the converted stable was shut. This she
had not considered in her planning. It loomed high and
heavy, its surface darkened by wetness and its brass fit-
tings rusted.

For the space of several seconds, she stood there with
her hands hanging at her sides, dreading the onslaught of
despair she knew would shatter her if she found that she
could not open the door. Then she reached for the padlock
that hung at its center point and yanked at it.

It came apart, and she felt her knees buckling under a
rushing flood of relief. She leaned against the door for a

moment and then pushed at it, using all the strength in her body.

There was the raucous squawk of old hinges as the thick slab of wood moved inward. She took a few steps forward, unable to see anything in the darkness. Then her vision became adjusted to the gloom. The formless shadows took shape, became her own car, Edith's limousine, the Volkswagen bus.

Of course it was there. She might have expected to find it in the garage, Rosemary thought impatiently. It was a prop in the drama Edith and the others had been enacting. She remembered the man she had seen driving it, had caught only a glimpse of. If he wasn't the one she believed to be Judge Jonathan Kalman, then he was a twin brother.

It was all becoming clearer now; some of the questions were being answered. And the odds were shortening. She had two chances of getting away—Edith's car, and the bus. In their haste and excitement, the people who had last ridden in the Volkswagen might have neglected to lock it and take the keys with them.

She was edging along the driver's side when she heard the noise. She stopped with her fingers on the handle of the door, the paralysis of fear holding her motionless. She tried to tell herself that she was imagining that sound, that there was no one in the garage except her. But then it came again, a faint thudding sound from somewhere beyond the bus, in the space between it and her own car.

Her first impulse, when life came back into her body, was to flee, to run as fast as she could out of this dark, ill-smelling place. She had taken only a few steps when a thought occurred to her, and she halted, went back to the bus, and edged her way cautiously to its other side.

"Drew?" she called softly. "Is it you?"

She peered into the narrow space between her car and the Volkswagen and saw the shape of something lying there on the floor. Creeping closer, she could make out the outlines of a body in an awkward, unnatural position.

When she bent down and touched him, she discovered why he had not been able to move or speak to her when she had called out to him. There was a gag in his mouth,

held there by strips of adhesive tape. A rope bound his ankles tightly, and his hands were fastened together behind
his back. The faint noise she had heard had been the striking of his feet against the floor.

There was scarcely room enough for her to squeeze past
her car, and she would not have been able to reach his
mouth; so she went around the front of the bus and forced
her way down to him from the other direction. She stretched a hand down to his face, grasped the corner of one
strip of adhesive tape, and yanked it away quickly. She
heard him moan and said, "This is the only way. It's worse
if you putter around with it."

He nodded, his eyes gleaming in the darkness. When his
mouth was free and she had removed the gag from it, he
gave a deep sigh. It was a moment or two before he could
speak.

Then he said, "You don't know what it's like to be able
to breathe again! I thought for a while there that I was
going to suffocate. What time is it? I must have been lying
here like this for hours."

She tried to look at her watch, but its tiny face was obscured by the darkness. When she lifted it closer and could
hear no ticking, she placed it against her ear.

"Stopped. I'm sorry. With everything else that's been
happening, I forgot to wind it. No matter. I'm going to get
those knots undone. Drew, did you get a chance to make a
stab at Edith's car or the bus? When did—this happen?
How soon after you left me?"

Immediately, he told her. He had come into the garage,
seen nothing except the three vehicles, heard no one.
"And then the roof fell in on me. It's true, you know,
about seeing stars. Someone must have come up in back of
me. All I felt was that one blow on the back of my head,
and everything in it seemed to explode."

He tried to pull himself up into a sitting position and
asked anxiously, "How are you doing with those ropes?"

"Not very well." She was panting with exertion, and her
hands were beginning to feel sore from the pulling at the
ropes and the unsuccessful effort to loosen the knots.

The terror that someone would come and find her there

with Drew started to creep into her nerves, and her hands began to shake until they were useless.

"I'm not getting anywhere, Drew." Her voice rose high and then cracked. "Do you have anything in your pockets? Something sharp—knife, perhaps?"

"Nothing like that. I didn't, you see, anticipate being in a position where I would need one. Careless of me!"

She knew that he was trying to keep his tone light because he must have sensed how close to the point of weeping with frustration she was. He made another attempt to pulled himself upward, but he fell back on the floor and remained there, silent, for a short period of time.

Then he said, "There must be something in this place. Scissors or shears. Hedge clippers—I'm sure I put them back when I pruned a few of the bushes. On that far wall. I seem to remember that I took them down that day. And I would have hung them there when I finished with them. Over there," he motioned with his head. "Beyond where Edith's car is."

She got up from her knees and moved in the direction that he had indicated. Edith's big limousine was almost flush with the wall. There was not enough space for Rosemary to squeeze past it. But as she stood in front of its monstrous hood, she could see something gleaming in the darkness.

"I see them!" she cried to Drew. "They're there, if I can only get at them."

She could think of only one way, and she pulled herself up over the nearest fender and crawled across the hood. She did not dare to try to stand up because she knew that, if she attempted it, her feet would slide on the smooth surface.

Bracing herself on her knees, she lifted one hand and reached for the shears. Her fingers were inches away from them. She cried out in annoyance as her knee began to throb.

"A little more time in this place, and I'll be a hospital case," she muttered; Drew, evidently hearing her voice but not what she was saying, called, "What's that? Honey, are you all right?"

She did not answer him, because she was intent on creeping further forward. She could hear him thrashing about in the narrow space where he was lying.

Stretching carefully, she managed to get her hand on the clippers and loosen them from their peg. Her fingers closed around a blade as they slipped down the wall, and she felt the heat of pain in her palm. But there was nothing but triumph in her voice as she shouted, "Got them! Drew! I'll have you cut free in a minute."

She went sliding down over the hood and landed lightly on her feet. She started back toward the Volkswagen, the clippers held tightly in her grip. Facing away from the door, she did not see the figure standing on the threshold. She did not hear the stealthy footsteps.

The intuitive sense that made her suspect that there was someone else in the garage sent her head turning toward the door. And then the blow fell, glancing off the curve of her skull behind her ear.

She sank down slowly, her last thought a foolish one: Drew was right. You did see stars. And tiny, bright, whirling spots. And pinwheels.

Chapter Twenty-Three

SHE CAME back to consciousness hearing Drew's voice. It sounded far away, vague, and she thought that she must have been dreaming. Of course this was only a dream. She was somewhere in darkness, and she could not move. It could only be one of those nightmares in which the mind seems to function but the body is trapped and useless.

Drew was calling her name over and over. The voice was louder now, and she knew that he was somewhere only a few feet away. She tried to sit up, but the awkward position of her hands behind her back kept her from rising. And when she attempted to pull them free, the ropes cut into her wrists like metal bands.

Her ankles were bound together, too. She discovered that when she tried to move them. Hands tied, feet bound together. But it was Drew who—

The line of thought snapped and was never finished. Where she was, and why, and what had been done to her dawned with ugly clarity in her brain.

She had been struck down as Drew had been struck down, bound, hands and feet, as he had been bound. There was only one difference: her assailant had not gagged her mouth or put the gag back in Drew's mouth.

In too much of a hurry? She was not able to accept that premise, and the true reason why their mouths had been left free sickened her with despair. It did not matter whether or not they could use their voices. Screams, shouts, screeching, calling—nothing would be heard by anyone who could help them.

Drew was still trying to get her to answer him. She could hear the scuffling of his feet as he attempted to push himself in her direction.

"Rosemary, are you all right? What happened? For God's sake, will you say something, girl?"

The throbbing had begun in her head, dozens of little hammers banging until she felt dizzy with the pain. But she could force out her voice and said, in as light a tone as she could manage, "They didn't want to discriminate against me, it seems. His and hers lumps."

Relief was making him testy. He growled, "Fine time for the jokes. You're tied up, too?"

"Very definitely. Trussed up like an animal waiting for the slaughter."

It had been the wrong thing to say. She realized that the moment the words were out, but there was no way to recall them. She added hastily, "Nothing but a figure of speech. We can't be in any danger. They don't actually mean to kill us. Because if whoever banged us on our skulls had wanted to, he could have made the blows a little harder. So you see—"

"I don't see anything of the kind," Drew interrupted grumpily. "They know what they're doing. The program runs like clockwork."

He had pushed himself out from between the two cars by that time. She could see his figure, at first formless, then a shape with its outlines blurred. His face was a pale oval, featureless until he came closer to her, inching himself along like a baby not yet able to walk but finding its own way of locomotion.

When he was beside her, he said grimly, "Might as well face the truth. I could lie to you, darling; I could tell you not to worry, that I'd get you out of this somehow. But I won't, because I can't. I'm not the superhero who rescues the fair maiden. You know how desperate they are, don't you? And why?"

She did not want him to go on talking any longer. She could sense that he was exhausted from his long confinement in this malodorous place, alone and with only the companionship of his fear-inspired thoughts.

He asked, his voice hoarse and abrupt, "What happened to the clippers?"

"I must have dropped them. They must be here on the floor somewhere. Drew, do you think—"

"No," he said frankly. "I can't perform miracles. But I can sure as hell try. If I can manage to get one of my wrists against one of the blades, maybe I can saw the rope off. Where do you think you dropped them? About where would they be?"

She told him that she had been carrying them back to him, and had her back to the door when she was struck down. And that in that burst of pain and brightness, she had thrown up her hands. She had not heard the shears strike against the cement floor.

"I must have been knocked out the minute that thing, whatever it was, hit me."

"No need to apologize," he growled.

"Well, I'm not!" she began and then stopped speaking. What a time this was for a quarrel, she thought. She could not see his face now. It was turned away as he bumped himself in the other direction, but she sensed he was probably grinning. And she was aware of what he was trying to do: divert her mind from the hopelessness of their situation.

It was hopeless. He was not going to find the clippers there in the dark. And if, by any chance, he did, it was impossible for him to cut away the ropes around his wrists with a blade that was probably too rusty to serve any purpose.

But he did find them, and he shifted his position. And he said, on a soaring note of triumph, "They're open! Now if I can get one hand around them and hold the other in front of the blade . . . Damn! It isn't going to work!"

He was to despair a dozen times within the next half hour. She could see him squirm and shift, stop moving to take long, ragged breaths. He muttered and groaned, swore, apologized curtly for the language he was using, and went back to what he was trying to do, stubbornly and steadily.

And at last, panting, he said, "I've got it now! The tip of the blade under the bottom rope. If I push against it, I think it will work. It'll take time. Don't expect that this is going to be a one-minute thing. Rosemary, you know how to pray?"

"Of course."

"Then start praying. I'm a little out of practice."

He was silent for a long time. She could hear the sound of the steel against the rope, Drew's heavy breathing, and her own.

Once she asked, "Are you making it?" and he snapped, "What do you want, a progress report?"

A moment later he said, "Sorry! This isn't exactly the right sort of deal for quieting the nerves. Maybe if I rest for a while, my disposition will improve."

Then he asked, "Why don't you try to push yourself up against the wall, and rest your back against it? You'll be more comfortable. Seems you're going to be waiting for a good long time."

She did as he suggested, moving inch by inch, digging her heels against the concrete until she could finally lift her body, turn, and slump against the surface of wood.

"You're right," she gasped, and thought to herself that it had been an exercise in futility. What difference could it possibly make whether or not she was comfortable? Edith and her little band of friends were not going to let her and Drew escape that easily. Even if Drew managed to get his hands free, there was no way for the two of them to get away from Farview.

The thing about the car keys had been unrealistic, wishful thinking. They would not have been carelessly left behind. In the drama that had been played, and was still being played, every small detail had been planned precisely and carried out with care.

"Drew!" Rosemary called across to him, and he turned his head. "There's only one thing I don't understand about all this. Edith wanted so badly for me to come here. She was glad to see me. Why, if I wasn't in the way of her getting all of her father's estate, did she want me here? She knew there was no money, so that couldn't be the reason. It's the only thing that doesn't fit."

He didn't answer that. He muttered something that sounded like, "We may never know."

And he changed the subject so suddenly that Rosemary was bewildered.

"Honey, do you ever go bowling?"

She repeated the word in a stunned voice. Then she asked, "What in the world has that to do with anything?"

"I was just thinking about it. I went one night with a bunch of guys from the office. There was this couple using the next lane. The girl was about your age and a rotten bowler. Half of her balls went down the gutter. The man with her wasn't all that great, either. But every time he'd knock down a few pins, she'd let out a little cry like he was the champion of the world. And when they were finished, I caught a look that passed between them," Drew said softly. "It was a special kind of look, as though they were pouring out what they felt for each other. They were in love, and it was in their eyes."

He was speaking in a tone that she had never heard him use before—sober, wistful, a little sad.

"I thought then how great it would be if I'd had a girl who looked at me that way. Who'd go bowling with me and think everything I did was better than anyone else could do it." He drew up a deep sigh before he went on. "When I saw you again, the kid who'd been my friend before we grew up, I knew I'd found what I didn't know I was looking for. Not that there was anything starry-eyed about you. Which was, of course, my own damned fault. I acted like a donkey. I teased you and irritated you. In short, I blew the whole thing."

"Drew, please don't! Not here, not now," she begged in a breaking voice.

"Then when? It won't do any good to say that we're going to get out of this, and that I'll have a chance to lead up to it gracefully, say the proper things at the right time. I'm not a graceful guy, my darling. I'm sarcastic and mean-tempered, and I get a kick out of getting a rise out of people. This sounds like a final confession," and he barked a laugh. "But for what it will mean, I want you to know the truth about me."

There was a short pause. Then he said, "Because I've fallen in love with you. And if we ever do get out of this, I'm going to ask you to marry me. Nothing but the total commitment is good enough. Don't answer me now," he commanded harshly and hastily as she tried to speak. "This is a false situation. You might feel sorry for me, mistake that for something else. I don't want you to say something you wouldn't mean under normal circumstances. Or tell me anything you'd rather keep to yourself."

Then, in exasperating contradiction, he demanded, "You haven't fallen for that guy Edith's got hidden away in the ell—that Martin Morse?"

Rosemary said shortly, "No, I have not. Drew, do you think they'll come back soon? Whoever they were who knocked us out and tied us up like this?"

That seemed to remind him of what he had been trying to do. He began to saw the blade of the clippers against the ropes once more. It took him a little while to answer.

"Not yet. They're all too busy getting drunk in there. The celebration party won't be finished for some time."

He was wrong. It was only a few minutes later when Rosemary heard the garage door squeaking open.

Chapter Twenty-Four

THE BEAM from a flashlight stabbed into the darkness of the garage and wavered for an instant; then Rosemary heard the unsteady feet that stumbled on the threshold.

She pushed herself further back against the wall, although she knew, even stunned by terror as she was, that it was useless. Whoever was holding the flashlight would find her in that strong shaft of brightness. There was no escape. Someone had come to finish the job that had been started when Drew was struck down in this isolated, deserted place.

He seemed not to be breathing. When she turned her head in his direction, she saw the rigidity of his body. She ached to be able to speak to him, to tell him that his story about the two young people in the bowling alley had moved her and that she did not care that he was graceless and blunt and totally without superficial charm.

And what a fine time for me to find out that I'm in love, she thought, with the stinging of tears behind her eyelids. But she had no time to think of anything else, because the man—it had to be a man, she realized, for the footsteps were heavy—was moving further into the garage, playing his flashlight around in an uncertain sort of way.

Then Rosemary heard the other footsteps, light as they were. They came rushing down the path that led from the driveway, sloshing in the rain-soaked earth. She heard, too, the calling voice, breathless and with notes of fury in it: "Charlie! Charlie!"

The shaft of light swiveled and disappeared. Rosemary could see nothing from where she was, pressed back against the wall; but she recognized Edith's voice when the woman demanded, "What are you doing here? I told you we couldn't do anything about them until he went to bed. The lights are still on in his room. You want to blow it all, is that it?"

The man answered her in a mumble. Rosemary heard only a few words: "cute little chick . . . don't expect me to live like a monk, do you? . . . the rest of you old hags . . . "

Edith was becoming shriller, her rage mounting. "So that's it! You're drunk and on the prowl for a little romance. You fool! A pretty face, and you lose your mind! I don't care what you do when you're not here, but you're not going to spoil things for the rest of us."

She stopped shouting and gasped a few ragged breaths. Then she said, more quietly, "You know what I've got planned for her. And it was working. He saw her. He talked to her. It would have all worked out if that miserable, snooping stepson of mine hadn't tried to throw in the monkey wrench. Well, it's not too late. I'll get them together before the night is out."

"Very pretty." The man was trying to sneer, but his voice was thick and so the effect did not quite come off. He seemed to be whining. "It all has to be your way, glorious leader! The haul this time wasn't enough for you. Madame Greed personified." He stumbled over the last words: "Thash you!"

"Sober up, for God's sake. We've got work to do tonight, when his lights go out. Then I'll wake him up, after we take care of that rotten kid his father wished on me. Come on, Charlie, let me take your arm. We'll go back to the house. You probably need to rest up for a while."

"Need 'nother little drink! You'll let me have 'nother little drink?"

Edith did not speak for a moment or two. Then she said coaxingly, "After you've had something to eat or a cup of coffee. I need your help. We've all got to stick together.

I'll let you get him into the boat. You can take him out
into the middle of the bay."

"No, you don't. Think I'm too drunk to know what's in
that scheming mind of yours?" His voice was sly, and the
words were interrupted by a chuckle. "Don't trust you,
Edie girl. It'd be a trap, thash what it'd be. I'd end up like
Pete."

She snapped, "Pete died a natural death, you know
that. You were there. He went under in a heart attack.
Nobody had anything to do with it. If I'd had the slightest
suspicion . . ."

The man began to snivel. The tearful drunk, Rosemary
thought. The assaults of self-pity, the aggrieved feeling.

"Buried in a strange place, far away from his loved
ones."

"He had none," Edith said shortly. "Like the rest of
you. I didn't pick anyone who had loved ones that they
might feel sloppy enough about to confide in. What difference does it make where he was buried? We had to get
him out of the way with no questions asked about where
he died and how and all that. Enough of this, my friend.
We're going back to the house."

The voices began to grow fainter as they moved out of
the garage. Charlie started to say, "We could put a match
to this place; we're taking chances with both of them still
alive." But Edith cut him off quickly.

"You are a fool. You couldn't start a fire in the rain.
Besides, it has to be the way we planned. He goes out in
the boat and she'll fall into Morse's arms when she finds
herself alone."

There was no more. There was the sound of the door
closing, and then the silence fell. Rosemary waited for
Drew to speak, but when he did not, she said, "Drew?
They didn't look to see if we were still here! Wouldn't you
think that they'd have at least checked? How could they
have been sure that we hadn't gotten away?"

He laughed shortly. "Over-confidence. It happens to
the best of them. If they'd taken the trouble to find out,
they'd have seen that you'd managed to take the tape off
my mouth. And that I'd been sweating to get that blasted

tool to do some good. Well, back to the grind. I think I'm making some progress. The blade has broken part of the rope."

A little while later, while he was still busy, Rosemary asked, "What did you make out of all that? What they were saying, I mean?"

He stopped sawing long enough to answer her. "That she's trying to cook up something between you and Morse. And that what's waiting for me is a ride in the speedboat from which, it seems, I don't return. One-way trip."

Rosemary, her heart feeling high in her throat, whispered, "They wouldn't! At least they're not murderers. That man they spoke about—Pete, wasn't it?—evidently died naturally, in a heart seizure. He must be the one buried in the lawn. Naturally," she repeated slowly and softly. "Edith didn't say he'd been hanged. So who was it that I saw? The one that looked like Roland Harmon?"

There was no reply from Drew. He was grunting with exertion. She could see the movement of his body as he pushed it back and forth more rapidly now, with stronger motions.

Time went by in what seemed to Rosemary like slowly moving hours. She thought about Martin Morse, up in his closed-off rooms, and remembered what Edith had said about him. For some reason that she could not understand, it was he who was delaying the carrying out of what came next for her and Drew. Because his lights were still on. Because Edith was waiting for him to put out his lights so that he would not see what was to happen out on the grounds or on the ocean beyond them if he chanced to look out the window. Now Rosemary realized the reason for the delay.

Exhausted, afraid, her nerves stretched tightly, Rosemary began to giggle foolishly. Drew turned his head and growled, "So what's the big joke? I could use a laugh too, right at this point."

She quavered, "Edith may not know that Martin likes a lot of light around him. I think he's one of those people who can't bear to be in the dark. Maybe he even has to sleep with a lamp burning, and Edith—Edith might not be aware of that. And there she is waiting—"

"Real funny," Drew muttered. "That's what you're getting hysterical about? You know quite a lot about the golden boy, don't you?"

"Oh, Drew, don't let's start fighting," she begged. "Not now."

He went back to what he had been doing, and only a few moments later he burst out, "Got it! I knew if I stuck with it long enough it would give."

He was making scuffling noises with his feet, and although she could see him only dimly, she knew that he was bending forward and untying the ropes around his ankles. It was not accomplished easily, but he came over to where she was sitting against the wall a short time later. He threw away the pieces of ropes he was holding and slid down on his knees beside her.

"You've been patient, dear love," he said. "Better than I'd have expected. I'd have thought you'd throw hysterics, weep and wail and carry on like crazy."

She looked down at the top of his head as he struggled with the knots. "If that's meant to be a compliment, it didn't quite come off. But I thank you for the effort—I think."

"I'm taking none of that sort of talk from you, my fair Rose. There are certain ground rules, and I'll expect you to follow them. I'll lay them down later, when we have time. Right now, the thing is to get out of here."

"And then?"

"One thing at a time. I'm getting down that road if I have to carry you on my back. Which, it seems, I may have to."

He had put her on her feet, and he grabbed her as she swayed. One of her feet was asleep, and when she placed it on the floor, sharp tingling needles shot through it. Her ankles and wrists were sore where the rope had bitten into them. And the dull throbbing started in her head once more.

"I'll be all right in a minute," she said unsteadily. "Right now I'm a mess, but I'll recover."

He kept his arms around her, and she leaned against him with her face in the hollow of his shoulder. When he asked, "You are my girl, aren't you?" her answer was muffled in his jacket.

"I can't make anything out of that," he complained. "Sounds like some kind of Bantu dialect. Hope we're not going to have trouble communicating."

So she had to lift her face and say that she *was* his girl, that there was no other man who meant anything to her, and that yes, she loved him madly, detestable creature that he was.

"I'll be satisfied with that for now," he conceded. "We'll let the rest of it go for a while. Come on!" And with his arm still around her, he led her to the door.

He put out his hand to pull it open. He yanked at the handle, tried to shake it, tugged. And nothing at all happened. The door remained fast.

Rosemary cried inanely, "We're locked in!"

And Drew said, his voice unsteady, "God, you're bright as well as beautiful!"

Chapter Twenty-Five

HE WENT on tugging at the door handle for another moment or two until Rosemary said, her voice catching on a sob, "It's not going to do any good! All this . . . getting us free . . . What use was that, when she could snap that padlock together and trap us in here?"

"You give up easily."

Drew moved away from her and began to prowl around the garage. She heard the light sliding of his footsteps, a little uneven, and she guessed that he, too, found walking awkward after not having used his legs for so long.

She tried to follow him, but when he heard her behind him, he whirled and rasped, "Stay where you are! We don't want another accident. You could trip over something."

So she remained where she was, standing in front of her car with her hand on its hood. It did not do anything to comfort her. It was not going to be the means by which she would get away from the horror and the danger. But it was hers, something familiar in this strange world in which she found herself, part of the saner world she had known before she came to Farview.

The hours in the garage, the fear and the exhaustion, the rising hope which had died such an abrupt death—all those things caught up with her suddenly. She leaned forward, her arms supporting her on the hood, and cried openly and without shame.

Drew came back. She expected that he would be angry with her because she had broken down. But he put his arms around her gently and lifted her up and pressed her face against his shoulder. He made murmuring noises deep in his throat and although there were no words that went with them, she understood that they were designed for solace.

"I'm sorry," she said when she raised her head. "It was —just that it all got too much for me. Now you know what a weak character I am. A coward. I ran away from what happened before I came here . . . Tommy Ross . . . Daria . . . having to look for another apartment."

"Spare me," Drew begged. "We're not going to go into that sad story again. And you're talking about the woman I love."

He kissed her lightly and briefly. Then, as he started to walk away from her, she asked, "What is it you're looking for, another way out?"

"There should be one," he told her. "When I came into the garage this afternoon—before someone conked me on the head and knocked me out—I heard something rattle, like glass. An old place like this must have a window. I'm not up on coach houses, they're before my time. But it seems that they must have been built well. People were fond of their horses, treated them well. The grooms, or whoever it was that took care of them, must have spent a lot of time in the stables. So why not windows? There was no electricity in those days. Even with the door open, they'd have needed more light."

It was a brave, forthright speech, but Rosemary didn't believe a word of it. She was not sure that Drew did, either. He might be trying to paste together the shattered hopes.

Since she expected nothing to come of his searching, her disappointment would not be as keen as his when he found no means of getting free. When he moved away from her, she felt the squeezing of pity for him. He was a man who could not accept defeat easily. She waited for him to burst out in frustration when he was forced to admit, at last, that there was no window in the garage.

What she heard, a very short time later, was a wild cry of triumph. "Told you so!" and he came back to her and took her hand and led her through the darkness.

The window cut into the far wall was dim and dusty, its glass almost obscured by the grime of many years. It was easy to see why Drew had not found it in his first trip around the garage. Rosemary could believe he had not imagined that rattling sound he had described. Its putty must have loosened; the old wood was doubtlessly warped.

Drew dropped her hand and put both of his on the crossbar at the point where the two long, narrow panes met. He pushed upward and nothing happened. "Locked!" he gritted. "Sure, it would be locked. But there's a fastener up here."

For a long time she could see his hand, pale in the gloom, trying to move the old-fashioned latch. She would have understood if he had relieved his feelings with words that could not be used in polite society. But he seemed to be in control of his temper. All she heard was the hissing of his breath between clenched teeth.

He turned finally and said, "I'll have to find something to smash the glass with," and he went away for a little while. She heard him in a far corner of the garage, sounding as though he were rummaging around there.

He came back with something in his hand, but there was not enough light for Rosemary to see what he carried. He told her it was a tire jack.

"And if it's strong enough to hold up that old crate of Edith's, it'll do the trick. But stand away back. One good crack should do it. Get out of the way of flying glass, my accident-prone love."

She tried to ask him if it would not be dangerous for him, too. And why didn't he find something to wrap around the jack before he crashed it against the window? He growled that she had seen that in the movies and that he wasn't going to waste time searching for anything else.

Back beside her own car again, she heard the splintering of the windowpane, loud in the silence. After that, there were lighter sounds, and above them she could hear Drew's voice. He told her that he was clearing the frame of the shards of glass so that he could climb through it. Their tinkling went on for a little while as they hit the ground outside the garage.

"And you're to stay right where you are," he ordered, "until I get the door open. You're not to move, understand?"

There was a final clinking sound and, a moment later, Drew's footsteps were sloughing through the wet ground outside. The padlock on the door began to rattle. He was not finding it easy to open, she knew, and there was a long waiting period, at the end of which she was sure that she would have to climb out the window as Drew had done.

But the door was pushed open suddenly, its rusted hinges squeaking. Drew's voice was shouting to her to hurry, and she saw the narrow shaft of brilliance stabbing into the garage. It moved until it found her, and she was blinded by it and stopped to throw her hands over her eyes.

She did not want to see who was holding the flashlight. Fear and despair were sending a cold, rushing flood through her veins. She stumbled as the beam moved away from her, and then Drew was at her side, his free hand fastening around one of her wrists.

When she could speak again, she choked, "You scared me half to death. I thought it was—was him come back!"

"He must have dropped this outside." Drew was leading her toward the door. "And the rain's stopped. Another break for us. Honey, we're going to make it now. We'll take it easy down the road. Stop whenever you get tired and rest. You're not too badly off, are you?"

He lifted the torch to a point where he could see her face without bedazzling her eyes. And then she saw it—the smears of blood on his fingers and the pool of it that hid his wrist. Little red streams ran along his arm into his sleeve.

"You're cut!"

She sounded stupid and stunned. She could not wrench her eyes away from the sight of his bleeding wrist. Numbed, she scarcely heard him when he said, shame-facedly, "There was one piece of glass I didn't see."

He lifted the flashlight and moved its beam over her face. "You're not one of these women who faint at the sight of blood, are you?" he asked anxiously. "I'm all right, darling. I could use something to wipe this off with, though. I don't seem to have a handkerchief with me. How about you?"

Still frozen, but with physical sickness squirming inside her, she managed to shake her head. She had left her handbag in her bedroom. There was nothing in the pockets of her raincoat. Hysteria of fear, a new kind, was shaking her. Drew might slough off his slashed wrist as unimportant, but all she could think of was that he would doubtlessly bleed to death if she did not help him.

Her own hand was blotched and red and sticky now. She could see it in the ray of light. She pulled it free and ran to the open door and through it. She heard him behind her as she raced up the path and made the turn at the driveway in the direction of the house.

She had not been aware that she was screaming. The sound seemed to come from somewhere far away. But her throat was raw and aching by the time she reached the steps.

Drew caught up with her there. His hands clamped around her shoulders and he shook her.

"You little nitwit! They'd have to be deaf in there not to hear you!" She knew that he was furious with her. She tried to speak, but no words would come. Then he pulled her away from the steps. "You've ruined everything! We'll never make it now!"

She began to babble about his bleeding to death as he dragged her toward the driveway. She was conscious of pain from the grip of his fingers but she tried to control the shuddering that was making her feet useless. She had taken only a few steps when the area around the house flared into sudden brilliance.

The light poured out from the big door beyond the porch, from the rooms on the first floor, from a strong bulb over a side entrance.

And then the grounds were full of people. They came racing through the entrance door, jostling each other in their haste, shouting and crying out in a Babel of voices.

Rosemary saw them as figures in a nightmare, wavering and ghostlike as they ran through the light and then into the shadows. They surrounded the two who stood on the driveway, their arms around each other like actors under a spotlight.

And then Edith came, moving leisurely and gracefully down the stairs. When she was a foot or two away from Rosemary and Drew, she asked, with a curious note in her voice, "You did not really think you could get away, did you?"

Chapter Twenty-Six

ALTHOUGH THERE was a strong smell of liquor about her, she was, of all of them, the most completely sober. The man who stood behind Rosemary was shuffling his feet and mumbling incoherently. The faces of Lucinda and Bertha Swift, who had not come very far into the circle, looked slack. The others had staggered a little as they came running down the steps.

But Edith was cool and in command of herself. When Rosemary lifted Drew's hand to show her aunt the bleeding wrist, there was a sharp, imperious command.

"Charlie, give him your handkerchief! We don't want to lose him this way. And not yet."

The man tottered forward and took out the triangle of linen from his breast pocket. Rosemary saw his face then. It was the rather hard-featured face she had seen when he was with the others in the ell, and which she had believed was that of Judge Kalman. There was no resemblance at all now. He was wearing no makeup, no disguise, and he did not look like the missing judge or the man she had believed to be her grandfather.

He was an actor, as the younger, slimmer man was an actor. Nor did he now look anything like Jared Dana, the movie star who had died in a car crash, except for the lock of hair that fell over his forehead.

Rosemary, still dazed and not quite able to understand what it all meant, turned and glanced at the four women who stood a little space away. The one with the high cheekbones she picked out as the actress who had been impersonating Chotsie Metcalf. The woman beside her had some slight resemblance to Jennifer Myatt, the house-

157

wife who had been shopping on the day she had disappeared.

It would have been easy to mistake them all for the people they were portraying when she saw them in the dimly lit room in the ell.

Bertha and Lucinda Swift—Rosemary could not figure out what part they were playing in the drama which Edith had evidently staged, produced, and directed.

Like characters in a play, they stood about now as though waiting for their cues. A little intoxicated they might all be; but, she thought with a twisting of wryness, they were troupers to the end. The show must go on.

Charlie had bound up Drew's wrist and, Rosemary saw in the brightness of the lights, had done a good job of it. The handkerchief made a neat bandage, and he had picked up a small, sturdy piece of branch and made a tourniquet of it so Drew would not bleed to death. He was being saved for another sort of demise. Edith had been watching the bandaging and the twisting of the tourniquet, and when it was finished, she went closer to Rosemary and said in a throaty voice, "My dear, I am very sorry that things have turned out this way. Tell me, if it had not been for him," and she gestured toward Drew, "would you have fallen in love with Martin?"

Rosemary, her throat constricted so that nothing could come through it, shook her head. Edith stared at her for a moment, then lifted her shoulders and dropped them in a shrug.

"A pity! He couldn't help have been attracted to you. Not when you're so much like the wife he lost. I thought if I brought you here and he saw you, he'd see the resemblance. She was your type—small and delicate and helpless-looking. That's how she was, you know. She appealed to his protective instincts, and I was sure that if you thought you needed protection, you'd turn to him."

Rosemary found she could speak at last. She burst out, "You didn't, Aunt Edith! You wouldn't have done all those horrible things to me: made me think Grandfather was still alive, hung the body of that man from the tree, left the grave there for me to fall into! What could you have gained by all that?"

Without seeming to hear her, Edith went on speaking. "There were so many women, all of them throwing themselves at him and none of them knew that the only kind of woman he could have fallen in love with was someone who made him feel like something other than a bank account. I'm sorry."

Charlie, who had moved apart from the others, honked a brief laugh. "Your little scheme went off the track, Madame Greed. You had this idea that if you got your niece married to the millions, you'd be sitting pretty."

She admitted it calmly. "When you're up against it, as I was, you'll try anything. The other—well, we could have gotten away with it for just so long. I knew he'd be generous if I brought the two of them together. He might even," she added wistfully, "have made a settlement with me."

When she stopped speaking, a wave of sound seemed to spread among those who were listening, moving from one to the other until they were all clamoring. It was as though they were catching from each other some sort of disease of discontent and anger.

There were screeches of complaints from the women, deep mutters of rebellion from the men. Rosemary, turning her head first one way and then another, heard words and phrases that made her blood turn ever colder. ". . . not getting enough . . . don't divide it up fair . . . taking all the chances . . . "

And Bertha Swift cried out, her voice louder than the rest, "I had the chance! I should have put her out of the way! But you didn't want her killed, you said. Just make sure she slept long enough so she wouldn't know what was going on!"

Her sister chimed in, "Who's to say she won't go running to the police, now that she does know?"

Edith stepped backward and threw up her hands for silence. She looked somehow majestic, in spite of her wind-tossed hair and the sickly pallor of her skin.

"You will listen to me!" she cried. They grew quiet, although their expressions remained sullen. Rosemary moved closer to Drew, and he slid his arm around her waist and held her against him. They stood like that while Edith spoke in the trained, beautiful voice that might have moved any audience with its husky, throbbing notes.

It was theatrical in its cadence, and the others listened, seeming almost spellbound.

"Who was it who planned these things, right from the start? Who sought you out in your seedy little hotel rooms and apartments when you had nothing better than the unemployment line? Who chose you for the parts and showed you how to become something different? You never knew that my first husband was a makeup artist, but it was true, and I got that much from him if nothing else."

She let her voice sink to a dramatic pause, and then she smiled at them, a forgiving smile. She was in complete command of them, and the faint little hope that Rosemary had felt stirring died before it had a chance to kindle.

They were not going to rebel. No one was going to save her and Drew from whatever Edith was planning to do with them. Mutter and complain as they might, she was the leader, the brain, the driving spirit.

Drew murmured, in something like admiration, not seeming to realize that he was speaking, "What a performance!"

Edith frowned at him, the star annoyed at being interrupted by a member of the audience. She wrapped her arms around herself and lifted her chin high.

"I was the one who sent Emily to do the casing, because she has an aristocratic look and would not have looked out of place. And the house here!" She lifted her arm and waved her hand in a backward motion. "Where else would there be for such a perfect hideout? Miles from everywhere. And the ocean, the boat! And who found the fence in Canada, not even a hundred miles away—a couple of hours' drive?"

She faced them with a defiant toss of her head. "Now if anybody's got a squawk, let me hear it!"

Bertha Swift mumbled something under her breath, and Edith caught the sound of it.

"Speak up!" she ordered. "This is your chance. What's your beef?"

Bertha, the center of attention now, seemed to wish that she had kept still. Her feet scuffled on the damp grass. She made two false starts and broke off. She said finally, in the strained, careful voice of someone who had had too much to drink and was trying to sound dignified, "It was us who did all the dirty work. Cooking and cleaning and carrying up trays. If we'd given her too much of that stuff and she'd died, it'd have been us who'd have to take the rap."

Edith laughed; it was a little tinkling of derision. "That's fine, coming from you. If it hadn't been for me, you'd have had a choice of two things—starving or going on the streets. And you're not so young anymore, darling. You haven't had a part in anything since that soap opera half a dozen years ago," she finished with another cruel laugh.

There was movement among the others. They drew closer together uneasily, and Rosemary thought to herself, her own fear growing stronger, they were afraid of her. Whatever they had been in the theatrical world, they were amateurs in crime. And they would do whatever she said.

Then Edith spoke to them gently. She said, with a little throb of regret in her voice, "It didn't work out, what I'd planned for my niece and Martin. And so, you see, we must do something about her. We cannot simply let her go away because someday, perhaps not meaning to, she could say the wrong thing to someone. And we must go on with this until there is enough so that none of us has to worry about money again. And as for him," and her brilliant eyes stabbed through the light at Drew, "he signed his own death warrant the minute he drove up to the door. I knew he was snooping around, going down to Boston and staying overnight after the last job, playing Sir Galahad to my niece, being the big hero."

Rosemary pressed closer to Drew. It could not be real. She wouldn't let herself believe that. This scene under the lights, with the dark grounds as a backdrop, *was* a play of some sort, a frightening, frightful drama, with her and the man beside her as members of the cast.

Edith could not help acting, whatever the circumstances. With exquisite timing and with a soft, yet compelling voice for more stunning effect, she said, "And so they must both die!"

There was the beginning of a low cry from Drew, cut off sharply as though human hands had pressed suddenly at his throat. His hand was around Rosemary's and it tightened spasmodically and with such strength that the bones of her fingers felt as though they were cracking.

He lunged forward, not realizing that he still had his hand gripped around hers. She staggered and regained her footing in the spongy earth. All the physical things that had been plaguing her came back in clamoring assaults of pain. Her knee was throbbing. She could feel again the stinging in her wrists and ankles where the tight ropes had cut into her flesh. The hundreds of little drumbeats in her head pounded until she was dizzy with them.

After that one movement toward the porch, Drew stood swaying. He had lost blood, too much of it, and she knew that it had weakened him. There were two men, and in spite of the fact that they were both more than a little drunk, he would be no match for them. And there were five women, all of them with much at stake. Of all of them, Lucinda and her cigar-smoking sister were the tallest, the most raw-boned, looked the strongest.

Edith had known what she was doing every step of the way. She had let them have enough liquor to give them false courage, but not enough so that they would be unable to carry out her plans. She had stage-managed the whole thing and made certain that, when the time came to dispose of Rosemary and Drew, they would be where she wanted them. The two cars had been put out of commission. Then Drew had been struck and then another knockout blow had rendered the girl unconscious—everything working out step by step, leading up to this minute.

And we thought she might be careless enough to leave her own car keys where we could get them, Rosemary thought with a gurgle of hysteria. Drew's head turned, and he looked at her, his eyes deep and dark and glittering. She pressed his hand. There was nothing either of them could say. And Edith was speaking again in her rich, carrying voice.

"You and you," and she pointed at the two men in turn, "can handle him. You should have no trouble. A couple of you women, get hold of her. The boat will hold six. Charlie will pilot it as usual. No problems. Neither of them has anybody who'll come poking around and ask questions about them. And," she said, on a calm and matter-of-fact note that made what she was saying even more horrifying, "the coast along here is rocky. Not much chance of the bodies being recognized if they're ever washed up."

Drew's shout of protest came from down deep in his throat. As the two men began to move toward him, walking more steadily now, he tried to lift his arms. But they fell heavily to his sides, and Rosemary knew that he was still weakened by the loss of blood and that there was no hope at all of his evading his captors.

A quarrel had sprung up among the women. They began to bicker about who would go out in the boat. Lucinda sniffled that she was always seasick on the water; the girl who looked like Chotsie Metcalf snarled that she wasn't going to be the one to do the dirty work, that she drew the line at tossing somebody overboard.

There was a sudden silence, a cessation of movement so abrupt that the scene was like the breaking of an unwinding film. They stood frozen in stiff attitudes, hands half raised in angry gestures, their heads turned in the direction of the porch.

The man had called out one word: "Edith!" It was his voice which had barked, and it seemed to echo and crackle in the air. He stood with his figure outlined against the light at the open door, tall and straight and with the faint arrogance and authoritative manner that went with power and wealth.

Edith turned her head to follow the gazes of the others. She came back to life first. She laughed lightly on a deprecating note and said, in a fawning tone, "Why, have we disturbed you, darling? So sorry! Just some of my friends

who drove up; a little party. They were leaving right this
moment . . . ."

He walked slowly across the porch, and Rosemary
thought, still dazed in a sense of unreality, "Enter Martin
Morse, center stage. Other players turn in his direction as
he speaks."

"Don't take me for a fool, Edith! I heard it. I heard
enough. You will let that girl go. You didn't think I was
going to lose her now, did you, when she has just come
into my life?"

Edith drew up a long sigh and said regretfully, "So it
must be you, too, Martin! You've walked into this, and it
is too bad. But I cannot let you spoil things, either. We
can't turn back now. Charlie," she cried with a sweep of
her arm, "I'm afraid there'll have to be one more pas-
senger in the boat!"

When there was no movement behind her, she whirled
and screamed in fury. "You hear me, Charlie? We will all
be in the soup if you don't silence him! You have a gun,
haven't you? Use it!"

The man went weaving forward and crossed in front of
her. He was fumbling in his pocket as he reached the steps
and started up. And then he stopped, his body wavering,
and Rosemary saw the flash of brightness in Martin's hand
as he slid it quickly from behind his back.

He said sharply, "Don't you know that nobody in my
position would be without means of protecting himself?"

The gun was steady, and the sight of it seemed to con-
fuse Charlie. He made a false move, as though to climb
another step, and then reeled to one side. And without the
protection of his body, Edith was left there alone at the
moment that Martin Morse's gun exploded.

Chapter Twenty-Seven

THE SIGHT of Edith sinking to the ground with the red stain spreading near her shoulder was like the signal for a stampede. The two men and four women began to run in all directions, some of them sloughing through the wet grass toward the cliff that stretched up from the shore, others racing and stumbling down the driveway, all of them becoming lost in the darkness.

Only Rosemary and Drew remained where they had been when Edith was shot, the girl's hand in his tight grip. Then, as Martin moved woodenly down the steps, they walked slowly forward. Rosemary freed her hand and lowered herself to her knees beside her aunt.

Edith's wailing rose in waves of shrillness, then petered away to gulping sobs. She was weeping softly, her face drenched and puckered, while Martin stood and stared down at her with his mouth tightened and white.

"She won't die," he said at last He was still holding the gun, and he glanced down at it and tossed it away. He reached out and helped Rosemary to her feet. "I couldn't let her hurt you," he said simply.

Behind them, Drew growled, "We've got to get her into the house. You'll have to help me carry her, Morse. The police . . . ."

"Should be here soon. I called them while all this was going on. When I got onto what it meant." He turned and stared at Drew and asked, in a voice that was barely civil, "Who are you? I've seen you before?"

Rosemary told him. "If you heard it all, you should know. She said . . . They were supposed to . . . "

"Of course, the snooping stepson. The big hero," Martin said sourly. "Not thinking straight; I never used the gun before. It's not too bad a wound. With all your talents, Chester, you should be able to fix her up until the State Police get here. I thought they were the ones to call."

They carried Edith into the house and placed her on a sofa in the living room. Rosemary went to the kitchen and brought back a basin of hot water and towels. Edith was whimpering when Drew bent over her and washed the wound and bound her shoulder. Then she fainted. The three exchanged glances, now at a loss and all of them ill at ease.

Drew left the room abruptly, muttering about going outside to wait for the police. Rosemary took a few uncertain steps, intending to follow him. But Martin strode forward, put his hand around her arm, and turned her about to look into her face.

"What's he to you?" he demanded.

She was still a little dazed, and her tongue felt thick and swollen. She could not seem to speak, and his probing stare disconcerted her. He asked, still in that edged voice, "Somebody special?"

"Yes," she said finally. "I guess he is."

"And what can he give you?"

She was confused, not understanding the meaning of the question. "What would he give me?"

"Dullness. Drabness. The kind of monotony that's the death of marriage. Forget him, darling!" He had picked up her hands and his fingers were working over hers. "There's nothing in the world you couldn't have—with me. Dearest, I couldn't spend all the money I have, not if we lived a couple of hundred more years. Anything you want, anything! I have a yacht, but it was never much fun without the right person. I know where I can lay my hands on jewels as big and bright as your eyes. Paris, the Caribbean, a home in Switzerland—I'll buy you your own island. Anywhere in the world, anything you want."

He was growing hoarse, and when he stopped speaking, he was breathing unevenly. She drew her hands out of his clasp. She felt that he had never been refused anything at all during his entire adult life. The knowledge made her speak gently.

"I don't think I'd fit into a fairy tale very well. I'm not really the Cinderella type. And let's take a look at the truth, Martin. I'm not what you want. You don't even know me. It's all an illusion. You were here for a long time and you were lonely. And it seems—well, Edith said it, too. I'm a little like your wife, right? Some resemblance in looks? But that's probably all it was, just a look-alike thing."

He would have gone on arguing, but she backed away and went out to look for Drew. He was standing on the porch, his arms folded and his gaze fastened on the lower end of the driveway. He did not turn when she touched his arm.

He didn't answer, either, when she said, "Drew?" Then, after drawing up a long breath, she began to say all the wrong things. She hadn't realized how they were going to sound, but having started, she rushed on with her one-sided argument.

"If it wasn't for Martin, we'd be out on the ocean by now—in it, more likely. The last thing in the world he wanted was to come out of the ell and face the world again right now. We owe him our lives."

At that point, Drew whirled and faced her. "And he's sending in his bill, isn't that the way it is? Don't think I blame you, my little friend. What woman could resist that, could help falling for her rescuer, even if she hadn't before?"

She tried to say, "Oh, no, Drew!" but the words were lost under his crackling voice.

"To say nothing of his being loaded, somebody who's been fawned on all his life, been able to shower his women with anything their little hearts desired. Just think of all the things he could give you."

When he began to enumerate them, she moved away from him and said wearily, "I've just been through all this. Drew, I thought you'd understand."

"What's to understand? As for you, what's not to like? You'll never get another chance like this."

He stopped speaking, and his head swung in the other direction. Rosemary had heard the sound, too, the whining of a car motor from the road beyond the driveway. It grew louder in the stillness of the night, and there were others behind it. Their headlights threw shafts of sweeping brightness as they turned and came up the curve of the narrow path.

Rosemary and Drew talked to the police in the room which had been Henry Gilbert's study. There was a uniformed trooper who wrote down what they said in a notebook. Then he went away, leaving them alone with a tall, pleasant-featured man in a black raincoat. He did not sit down, but stood looking down at them when the questions were finished.

"I don't want to keep you too long," he said with a glance at Drew's wrist. "You'd better get that checked as soon as possible. Looks like an amateurish sort of bandage. Somebody from Division Four in Boston will be flying up. The latest job was in the Back Bay, one of those old firms that have been in business for generations. This crowd is wanted in New York, too, and a couple of other places. But the Boston boys get first crack at them."

"They escaped," Rosemary told him. "They ran away when my—my aunt was shot."

"And won't get far," he said easily. "This is a hard place to get away from. Matter of fact, a couple of them could have been picked up by now. They may try to take cover, but they'll have trouble on that score because they've left their stuff behind, their wigs and masks and makeup. And she was the brains of the gang. How about that! Fixing themselves up to look like people who've been out of it for years."

"They were stage people," Rosemary reminded him. "Actors and actresses that had been her friends."

Drew put in, "And it seemed like a clever ploy, on the surface. There were witnesses, but who'd believe them when they said they'd seen Jared Dana or Chotsie Metcalf or that man—that judge—holding up a jewelry store in broad daylight?"

The lieutenant nodded. "The pair of them, the girl in

the long blonde wig and the young fellow who was made up to look like—what was his name again, Dana? What a start they must have given the clerks in those stores! Like you said, Mr. Chester—in broad daylight. The boys from Division Four will have a job with this one," and he chuckled. "I'd like to see them trying to get witnesses to identify that gang."

"It was all an illusion." Rosemary spoke softly, almost to herself. "Everything, all of it. The one they called Charlie, he was fixed up to make me think that my grandfather was alive. The light in the room was dim and I hadn't seen Grandpa for a long time. Then there was the man hanging from the tree. They said he died from a heart attack," she told the lieutenant, "and perhaps that was true. What they did was hang his body there with his face made up to resemble Roland Harmon's."

Revulsion made her shudder. "He—he is, I think, in that grave I fell into, which might have been an accident. But the rest of the things weren't accidents. I was drugged or poisoned, perhaps both, so I wouldn't hear the cars coming back or the boat out on the water. Grandpa heard that too, and wrote about it in his journal."

After a moment of silence she said, with a little frown, "Those two women—Bertha and Lucinda Swift. I don't think they were part of the holdup gang. They were here most of the time. Where do they fit in all this?"

It was Drew who answered her. "They were playing their own parts—the Down East hired girls. In case, I imagine, somebody came up from the village. A delivery boy or a chance salesman, bill collectors, anyone like that. One thing is sure: all the bases were touched. That stepmother of mine had it all figured out."

The lieutenant said, "My men are searching the house. The haul from this latest job must be around somewhere. They wouldn't have had a chance to deliver it to their fence, whoever he may be. Well, that's something else for Boston to take care of."

He buttoned up his raincoat and seemed about to start for the door, then he stopped.

"There's this guy who shot Mrs. Chester. I didn't get

too good a look at him when the sergeant was taking him away, but he said he was—well, Martin Morse. It sounds fantastic," and he laughed briefly and apologetically, "another trick?"

"No." Rosemary did not look at Drew as she spoke. "That's really who he is. This is where he's been hiding."

"Is that a fact? The newspapers will have a field day with this one!" And he was chuckling as he raised his hand in a farewell salute.

Chapter Twenty-Eight

DREW SAID, "Wait here. I'll be back in a little while."

But it was not a little while, it was a very long time. Rosemary sat with her head against the back of the chair and her hands hanging limply at her sides.

She felt drained and drowsy, as though she had come awake after a particularly frightful nightmare which had left her in the grip of its memory. She tried to turn off her thoughts and make her mind blank, and when she succeeded, she began to doze.

The sound of footsteps outside the study brought her back to life with jolting suddenness. She pulled herself erect and saw Drew standing in the doorway. There was a twist of smile on his mouth, and he said dryly, "The resilience of youth! After all that's gone on, you can fall asleep."

She denied it hotly. "I was resting my eyes!"

"Try a new tack, girl. That's worn out. Your grandfather always used that one. He'd be sleeping like a rock, have to be shaken awake, and then he'd swear up and down that he'd only closed his eyes for a minute."

It did not sound at all like the old light-hearted raillery.

His voice was cold and distant. The stoniness of his eyes, before he turned them away, chilled her.

She asked, "What now?" and pulled herself out of the chair.

"Now we get out of here. One of the fuzz had a can of gasoline in his car. No problem with mine, it's outside now. We can take care of yours tomorrow."

He was still speaking cooly and impersonally. "Get whatever you need, and I'll drive you to a motel over on the highway. You can stay there for tonight. The detectives from Boston will probably want to talk to you in the morning."

Halfway to the door, she hesitated, and he said impatiently, "Well, come on! You hate to tear yourself away from this place?"

"I was thinking of Edith. She'll need someone. I suppose she's in the hospital by now. Shouldn't I—"

"No, you should not," he rasped. "She'd have had you dumped overboard without a qualm if he—Frank Merriwell in person—hadn't shown up in the nick of time."

She had never heard of Frank Merriwell, and she stared at Drew blankly. Someday she must ask him the significance of the name, someday when there was time and Farview had drifted away into the mists of memory.

And then, with a hard blow that struck at the region of her heart, came the realization that there would be no time in the future when she could ask Drew anything at all. There was not going to be any future for them together, or any shared memories.

She went upstairs, walking stiffly because she was still in the thrall of the pain. When she came down again, carrying a suitcase, Drew was standing at the foot of the stairs. He took the piece of luggage from her and put his other hand at her elbow. It was like the touch of a stranger.

She was helped into the front seat of the car and the suitcase went into the trunk. The car was moving down the driveway when she burst out, "This is ridiculous!"

He didn't turn to look at her. "Ridiculous?" he repeated politely.

"We're two grown people! We ought to be able to talk

together, say what we're thinking without sulking or being embarrassed. You told me that you were in love with me and that we'd be married if we ever got out of that mess. Well, we are out, and here you are acting like a . . . like a—"

She could not think of the right word, but it wouldn't have mattered anyway because Drew cut in before the end of the unfinished sentence. "That was when you were desperate enough to grab at anyone, before you got your chance at the golden boy."

Her voice crackled with rage when she cried, "Well, thank you heaps! It's nice to finally know what you think of me! And I might point out to you that there's no law against your calling Martin Morse by his right name. You seem to be afraid to do that. Martin Morse! Martin Morse!"

She kept saying it over and over again, until Drew removed one hand from the steering wheel and threw it up in a gesture of surrender. The car hit a bump in the road, and she was thrown against his shoulder. She righted herself with as much dignity as she could manage and her voice quavered all through the continuation of the tirade.

"It shouldn't be too difficult to say it if you try hard enough. And if you'll be polite and listen for a few minutes, I'll try to explain to you about Martin Morse."

She drew a deep breath. "He's a mass of neuroses, because he's rich and a lot of women have wanted to marry him. He never got over losing the one wife he had. You must know by now that Edith made this place available for him and, remembering what I looked like and seeing a resemblance between me and his dead wife, urged me to come here. She set up all those little tricks so I'd turn to him for protection. And that was designed to make him fall in love with me."

"And he did," Drew said softly.

"Not really, I think. He tried to transfer his feelings for Marianne to me. Do you want me to tell you everything he said when we were in the living room together?"

"Don't bother, I can guess. What I'm interested in is what you said to him."

She said pettishly, "I've got a good mind not to tell you. It isn't, actually, any business of yours at all." But there was no heat in the words, and after another long breath, she said, "Well, I guess maybe it is your business, because it would always be there between us and you'd never give me any peace until I told you."

So she told him, word for word, exactly what she had said to Martin and he to her. Drew listened in silence, his eyes fixed on the puddle-filled road. The only sound was the swishing of the tires and the noise of the waves grumbling on either side of the road.

When they reached Grist Mill Corners, the little village was asleep. No lights shone in any of the stores or cottages. Drew slowed down at the intersection and then turned right, in the direction of the highway. When they had reached it, he asked, "How about us spending an evening bowling sometime?"

The question and the mild tone of his voice startled her.

"How's that again?"

"Bowling. I want to see how you'll look at me when I knock down a couple of pins." Then, in an abrupt change of subject, "I've got an aunt in Connecticut, an eccentric old girl with the proverbial heart of gold under the crusty exterior. Seeing you have no place else to go, you can stay with her for as long as it'll take us to do the things you have to do before you get married. She's only an hour or so out of New York. Handy."

He was being high-handed again. She opened her mouth to protest, then shut it, realizing that she did not, after all, mind being bossed about by Drew.

"I'll be a rotten husband," he said cheerfully. "Jealous, overbearing, disagreeable, insisting on my own way all the time."

She added to the litany of his faults, "Rude, bossy, insulting, inconsiderate. And now, my dear future husband, you can stop playing the devil's advocate. I know what you are, and it seems that, for some reason or other, it's what I want."

He glanced into the rearview mirror and swore softly

under his breath because a truck was tailgating him and he could not pull onto the side of the road.

"You picked a fine time to tell me that," he gritted. "Did you choose this minute when I couldn't stop and kiss you? I'm going to make you sorry for that."

The truck passed them a little further along. Then Rosemary saw the garish sign in front of a motel, flickering through the hazy darkness and the tracing of neon light beneath it which said "VACANCY."

The car slowed down, turned, and slipped into the driveway where small units, all of them dark, formed a semicircle. There was a dim light burning in the office at one end of the crescent. Drew pulled up in front of it and stopped.

"This will do you fine for tonight. I'll be back first thing in the morning." And then his teeth flashed in a grin. "And now for you, fresh kid that you are; I never make idle threats."

He reached over and pulled her into his arms. His mouth was strong and hard against hers, and although she could have broken out of the embrace at any time if she had wanted to, she snuggled closer in his arms and put her hand against his cheek.

It was a long kiss. The clerk, who had heard the car stop, finally got up from his chair. He opened the door to look out, saw the two figures merged into what looked like one, and shrugged.

But his battered, disenchanted face was stamped with a foolish expression of surprise when only the girl came in a few minutes later and he heard the car pull away. She was walking lightly, as though on clouds, and her face had a shimmery, bemused look.

He handed her a pen and a registration card, and she cried, "Thank you!" as joyously as though he had handed her the world on a platter, he thought. Then he shrugged again, as though admitting grudgingly that life was still full of the unexpected.

How to do <u>almost</u> everything

What are the latest time and money-saving shortcuts for painting, papering, and varnishing floors, walls, ceilings, furniture? (See pages 102-111 of HOW TO DO *Almost* EVERYTHING.) What are the mini-recipes and the new ways to make food—from appetizers through desserts—exciting and delicious? (See pages 165-283.) How-to-do-it ideas like these have made Bert Bacharach, father of the celebrated composer (Burt), one of the most popular columnists in America.

This remarkable new book, HOW TO DO *Almost* EVERYTHING, is a fact-filled collection of Bert Bacharach's practical aids, containing thousands of tips and hints—for keeping house, gardening, cooking, driving, working, traveling, caring for children. It will answer hundreds of your questions, briefly and lucidly.

How to do <u>almost</u> everything

Is chock-full of useful information—information on almost everything you can think of, arranged by subject in short, easy-to-read tidbits, with an alphabetical index to help you find your way around —and written with the famed Bacharach touch.

SEND FOR YOUR FREE EXAMINATION COPY TODAY

We invite you to mail the coupon below. A copy of HOW TO DO *Almost* EVERYTHING will be sent to you at once. If at the end of ten days you do not feel that this book is one you will treasure, you may return it and owe nothing. Otherwise, we will bill you $6.95, plus postage and handling. At all bookstores, or write to Simon and Schuster, Dept. S-52, 630 Fifth Ave., New York, N.Y. 10020.

SIMON AND SCHUSTER, Dept. S-52
630 Fifth Ave., New York, N.Y. 10020

Please send me a copy of HOW TO DO *ALMOST* EVERYTHING. If after examining it for 10 days, I am not completely delighted, I may return the book and owe nothing. Otherwise, you will bill me for $6.95 plus mailing costs.

Name...

Address..

City....................State........Zip........

☐ *SAVE!* Enclose $6.95 now and we pay postage. Same 10-day privilege with full refund guaranteed. (N. Y. residents please add applicable sales tax.)